T0300622

Diagnosis of the Soul

Diagnosis of the Soul

The long road to the beginning

Richard Johns

authorHOUSE®

AuthorHouse™
1663 Liberty Drive
Bloomington, IN 47403
www.authorhouse.com
Phone: 1-800-839-8640

This is a work of fiction and the characters portrayed are entirely fictional.

First published by AuthorHouse   12/28/2011

ISBN: 978-1-4678-8199-9 (sc)
ISBN: 978-1-4678-8200-2 (ebk)

Printed in the United States of America

When he looked back over the past year he could barely comprehend how different his life now was. He had learned that ordinary did not have to mean mediocre. He knew this now but not back then, when it all began to change. In fact whenever Greg Finn was pressed into giving an opinion of himself for whatever reason, it would largely be derogatory in nature. He thought of himself as just an ordinary bloke, and was frequently overwhelmed by a lack of self confidence; a gibbering fretful timid ball of anxiety in most social contexts. At least, this was how he saw himself. Most people who knew him would certainly not describe him as ordinary.

He didn't look like a doctor—at least, that's what everyone told him, and when they did so he was never quite sure how to take it and indeed what was the correct response. Should he shrug his shoulders and just carry on, laugh in a light hearted and mildly amused fashion, or apologise and promise to alter his appearance in the fullness of time?

In the end he usually just took it as a form of compliment, deciding that on balance he would rather not conform to the generalisation of what a doctor tends to look like, or indeed should look like, which seemed in his experience to involve being towards the top end of the age scale, the top end of the weight scale, and possessing a large dose of superiority, pomposity and arrogance amongst the facial features. No, he was quite happy not looking like what he actually was, whatever that meant.

It seemed strange to him really, since he had wanted to be a doctor for as long as he could remember; way before he had any idea about what it involved or indeed much idea about anything at all, but nevertheless he was convinced that was what he wanted to be when he grew up. The trouble was he told everyone about this plan so often that he pretty much had to make it happen. He couldn't let Auntie Evelyn down who so longed to have a doctor in the family, even though her heart had already done so, or suffer the undoubted multitude of "I told you sos'" that were bound to ensue, so that even if it wasn't what he wanted to do anymore he was damn well going to do it anyway. Then he discovered how hard it was. And now, after all that hope, all that desire to succeed, all that endeavour to achieve his current status, he found himself hiding the title out of embarrassment for the image it portrayed.

To aid him in his long running battle for approval he was blessed with both the ability to actually enjoy exercise, which kept his body healthy, and was in the top 2% of the nation for intelligence, with one of those irritating memories (to everyone else) which required the absolute minimum of time input in order to digest large amounts of information, and more annoyingly still the added bonus of being able to process that information in a rational fashion. Not very ordinary indeed.

He was also humble, which was unusual in the profession and in fact almost got him kicked out of medical school, but he was able to save his career by managing to brag about how humble he was to the powers that be, who were reassured enough to allow him to continue.

However, it was neither of these attributes but rather his plain down to earthness and basic humanity which were key in allowing colleagues and patients alike to warm to him very quickly, all contributing towards making him into a rather excellent doctor.

Even though he didn't really want to be one anymore (and definitely not look like one).

He had excelled to an extent whereby he had succeeded from 87 candidates in being appointed the new partner at the Narcissus Group Practice in the heart of the city, in whose crumbling and pot-holed car park he now sat preparing himself for his first day. Partnerships were hard to come by, much prized and he had succeeded where the other 86 had failed, left to sift through the adverts for locum jobs or voluntary work overseas.

His natural reaction to the news that he had got the job was to think that he had fluked it. Somehow they hadn't spotted that he was just an ordinary bloke, and that everyone else were far more deserving.

Deep down he secretly hoped that he wouldn't get the job—yes, an extremely complimentary letter saying how very impressed they had all been and that under normal circumstances he would have been the ideal candidate, but unfortunately he had only just missed out on the partnership as the practice had realised that they had an urgent need for a Latvian speaking lesbian with a special interest in gynaecology to appeal to a worryingly expanding niche. Very sorry and good luck with your future interviews Dr. Finn.

Yes, that sort of letter would help to alleviate any implied shame in not getting the job that previously unheard of and definitely unexpected failure would undoubtedly arouse amongst family and friends. Those ones for whom blind faith was the order of the day; every day. Never mind the other 86 candidates about whom they knew nothing; no, he was bound to succeed because he always did. Yes, such a letter would have done nicely. But he did get the job.

He was aware he had been well and truly bullied into applying for this partnership by

Mrs. Finn, much as he had been bullied into marrying her in the first place; another partnership he had not really wanted. He only had himself to blame for colluding on both fronts, and blame himself he did. That was something he was really good at.

What he struggled to understand about himself was how he could manage to be robust, firm, competent and sure of himself in his work environment, with clarity of thought and excellent powers of reasoning and deduction, and to manage all that was thrown at him under conditions of extreme stress, but at the same time remain utterly pathetic when at home. He was ordered around, verbally abused, treated like shit, and just took it. And then hated himself for taking it, which made him feel more pathetic and more likely to take some more. The problem was that the thought of conflict with his wife was so abhorrent that he preferred to simply acquiesce on everything.

Mrs. Finn's motivation for pushing Greg into applying for the job in the first place was of a purely financial nature. She had seen the salary, and no other information was required. He was going to apply and damn well get it or else. It was high time she was kept in the manner that she at least knew she deserved, and after all, wasn't that why she had married him in the first place? She had locked onto him like a money seeking missile with an avaricious glint in her eye, sensing a good bet when she saw one. Forget all that sentimental nonsense about "love", that was for losers. He now belonged to her. He had been putty in her hands; utterly naive. He couldn't possibly have upset all those people she had already invited to the wedding before eventually letting him know they were getting married. So here he found himself stuck precisely where he definitely did not want to be. Sent out to bag the most lucrative job possible, this place had ticked the only relevant box. A six figure salary at only 27 years of age . . . well that would suffice for the time being. There had even been a mild thaw in the marital home at the news of his success.

There was of course a reason that the salary was so good . . . it was a total shithole.

Greg sat in his car and surveyed the alarming scene which presently surrounded him. He hated cities and here he was, right in the very centre of it all. The car park was situated around the back of the surgery and was actually a decent size, and was looked down on by a variety of neighbouring buildings. These seemed to be an eclectic mixture of architectural disasters born out of 1960s drug induced stupors, with a total lack of any aesthetic appeal thrown in for good measure. Buildings that made you cringe to look at them, that seemed to pollute the very air they stood in. Shapeless and soulless. Depressing. Enough to make you need to visit the doctor.

The car park itself was a minefield of potholes, and in addition was littered with a bewildering selection of random objects, which could really only have been thrown from the windows of those neighbouring buildings. Perhaps this was an entertaining way to pass some time; to alleviate the utter desolation of living in such a location by generating ones own amusing and entertaining game of land the potato in the pothole. Not only potatoes though, for there were many other vegetables present. Perhaps it had all started as a potato based game but they had simply exhausted the supply necessitating expansion into other objects.

There were certainly many different fruit and vegetables lying around the place, but also a selection of socks, underwear, a hat, and various magazines. Greg looked a little more closely. Yes, there were actual needles and syringes lying there on the ground, nicely scattered to tempt the inquisitive children attending the surgery that morning. Fantastic. This was obviously a recurrent issue since the practice had left a sharps box outside the main entrance, presumably so that anyone wishing to use this private car park for the purposes of shooting up would have a lovely safe place of disposal for their needles. This of course they then ignored, probably because they had just been shooting up.

Weren't the police meant to stop this sort of thing? Greg made a mental note to always tread carefully, and decided he could delay no longer, opened the car door and stepped out in a very gingerly fashion.

As he took his medical bag out of the boot he noticed the crowning stain on this sheet of filth—a used condom in the far corner, surrounded by beer cans. Yes, this completed the charming scene nicely. He wondered if the game devised by desolate neighbours had developed further into land the potato (stroke any fruit or vegetable of your choice) on the addict. And what a place to have sex!

"Where are you taking me tonight darling?"

"Oh, it's a wonderful place; great view of the stars, fresh food, easy access to medical care"

Greg remembered a distant dream of working amidst the beautiful English countryside, looking after a delightful rural population, and once again couldn't really understand how and why he had ended up here. Then he remembered . . . Mrs. Finn!

He got back in the car again. He didn't think he ought to wander in on his first day looking like he had just emerged from a war zone, so he gathered himself together. A member of staff emerged from a side door with a pair of grabbers and began picking up all the debris in a very matter of fact way, as if this was a typical part of her job. This explained why he had not noticed any such horrors when he had been for his interview. He listened to some Crowded House on the stereo which never failed to make him feel better about life, and tried again, but this time as if his surroundings were perfectly normal and just what he had expected.

The entrance of the new partner sparked a multitude of looks, glances, whispers and not a small degree of consternation amongst the rather numerous (and somewhat intimidating due to their number alone) reception staff and nurses gathered in the back office behind the front desk. He found himself the sole focus of a large number of feminine eyes, and felt quite unnerved, especially when he noted some actual drool appearing from the corner of one mouth. He could almost hear the ovaries bouncing around the various abdomens. Ovaries on the verge of shrivelling due to lack of sensory input, suddenly sparked into life by the mere presence of a potentially virile male, like when you are starving hungry and you put something with great flavour into your mouth and it makes your salivary glands explode, blurring the line between pleasure and pain. A sort of ecstasy grimace which he now found himself facing.

He was being scrutinised down to the smallest detail, and felt obliged to break the uncomfortable silence.

He smiled brightly, wished them all a good morning and insisted they all call him 'Greg'. This did not have the desired impact and in fact this morning triplet seemed to produce a somewhat strange reaction and not what he had intended at all. Indeed, he found himself checking that he was adequately zipped up.

It seemed his newly acquired employees were distinctly unused to being smiled at, surprised at being wished a good morning and had certainly never been asked to call a doctor by their first name before. He could have bounced in on a pogo stick, rhythmically farting the national anthem for all the reaction he received. He didn't realise it was simply shock on their behalf at being spoken to like ordinary human beings, which they were not used to at all. If he had shouted in a rude and abrupt manner they would have known where they were, but it was his, well, niceness. It took them all quite off their guard and none of them were able to respond in any normal fashion themselves. As a result Greg was left feeling bemused, and even embarrassed, and simply shuffled through the back office and reached gratefully for the door into the corridor, and thence to the door to his new room.

They watched him leave, spellbound, before shaking themselves down like they were coming out of some sort of a trance; and then the chatter started.

His own room. This four walled evidence that he had 'made it' if that was how you judge things. He barely had time to set his medical bag down on the large desk when there was a light knock on the door, and a member of staff walked through with a cup of tea. To most people this would not seem like very much at all, but to Greg this was a significant moment indeed. Throughout his medical career so far, nobody had ever brought him a cup of tea. People were always too busy, or stressed, or hadn't been on the appropriate tea making course. This simple pleasure gave him such a lift in mood to assuage his earlier misgivings. He tasted it. Strong and sweet . . . just how he liked it. How did they know?

He sat down in his black leather high backed chair and began to take in the surroundings. The room was large, airy, with high ceilings and a separate examination room, all fully equipped. It actually did feel quite grand.

Greg felt uneasy. It all seemed a little incongruous. The state of the neighbouring buildings, the car park, the reaction of the staff to normal polite behaviour, then the large grand room. Then he noticed the new gold name plate on the still open door, glinting in the reflection from the corridor lights. It just didn't seem to feel quite. He wondered when they would expect his pound of flesh.

He began to familiarise himself with the computer system, which would no doubt be his nemesis for some time to come. He struggled to make progress due to the succession of introductions which followed, as the staff came by individually to say hello. Without exception they seemed at first appearance to be extremely pleasant and deferential, and all steadfastly called him 'Dr. Finn'.

Again Greg was surprised by the level of pleasant normality not previously encountered in his own NHS experience.

Greg's pleasant surprise was mirrored by the reaction of the staff to their new doctor. He had created quite a significant stir behind reception. There was talk of some long awaited and much needed 'eye candy', his youth, his actually quite decent dress sense (they were used to seeing their male doctors in ancient stained trousers, shirts which used to be white but were now various shades of grey, and footwear that really belonged in a care home), and not to mention his physique. Again their experience to date was of excessively bulging guts, proudly displayed as if evidence of success, yet here they had someone who clearly kept himself in good shape. They were also surprised by Greg's apparent friendliness, and, well . . . normality.

They were so unused to such characteristics that there was even speculation that he was a plant; a trick by the partnership to catch them out, to lull them into a sense of false security so that they might let down their guard and do something criminal like try to talk to a doctor as an equal.

The fact was that none of them had experience of a doctor behaving like a reasonable human being before, and as such there was a collective resolve to take care, and keep several beady eyes on him at all times. Yes, they would have to watch him very closely to make sure he was genuine, only occasionally straying to his check out his pert rear end of course.

In stark contrast to the reception he received from reception was the very obvious lack of presence of any of his new partners. They had seemed friendly and welcoming at the interview, but their absence was so conspicuous, particularly in comparison to the welcome he had otherwise received, that it was a little worrying for Greg. He began to wonder if he had turned up on the appropriate day, and secretly hoped that he might be too early and have to go home for a while, say several years.

Meanwhile, elsewhere in the building, the other doctors were gradually filtering in as usual, each caught in their own little world, all having forgotten that their new partner was starting work today. This would not be altogether surprising if you were aware of the fact that individually they were each entirely convinced that they were the single most important person on the entire planet, and that very little existed of any importance at all unless it was of their doing. Of course, they were all quite adept at taking the credit for other peoples ideas; seamless acquisitions to flatter the ego, which aided the delusion.

It was remarkable how such people had gravitated together in one general practice partnership. They were all utterly convinced that only what they said mattered, and amazingly, were able to work together without coming to blows, since when any of them disagreed with each other it simply didn't register. They were just not aware of the disagreement, and carried on anyway. Their individual egos were all saying the same thing, so they were never offended by each other, as they just didn't recognise anyone else's opinion. This should simply not work. It seemed so unlikely, but actually this was probably the only circumstance where any of them could work with other human beings without being beaten to a pulp within a few microseconds.

If you were able to watch them as on some secretly filmed documentary, you would assume that the only reason they came in to work was so that they could then leave again. Go in to get through the day, to come home, get through to bed time, get up, get through another day, get through to the weekend, another week out of the way, soon be my holiday, just get through the next few weeks, then at last its here, its my holiday, must do something lavish to show to other people how successful I am, then tell everyone all about it to confirm this to anyone who will listen (and myself), then go to work to get through the day, to go to bed, then get up and get through another day, only eight weeks until Barbados, where I can tell anyone who will listen about what a great service I do for the community. Just got to get through these bloody patients first.

It was with a real and genuine sense of calling, of duty, and a desire to make a difference, to have a positive impact on the lives of other people, that Greg turned to peruse his first morning surgery as a partner. No longer the trainee, the junior, now the real thing. Of course with this came the responsibility, and with this came the fear. More than anything though, the overwhelming sensation was of excitement that here he was about to start seeing his own patients, by himself, using all the skills and knowledge he had acquired over many years, and that he had no idea what would walk through the door. This was what had drawn him to be a generalist; that you could never predict what you would see in your surgery. The constant challenge, academic, social and practical.

He was a little perturbed to find that he had already amassed 24 patients to see, and particularly when the telephone lines had only been switched on eleven minutes previously. It was half past eight, and he was supposed to be finished in around three hours time so that he could start on his home visits. That gave him around seven minutes per patient, and the list was still growing. Indeed in the time it took for him to work this out, a further two patients had been added to his list. A very scary deep sinking feeling threatened to overwhelm him, and he felt a wave of anxiety burst through his insides. How could he possibly consult all those patients in a thorough and professional manner in the time he had? But then they were all either here already, or on their way down, all expecting to be seen, to have their own particular problems resolved by the doctor; by him. What could he do but just get on with it and see what happened. He had been under severe pressure many times before in the hospital, but he had hoped it would be different here. He cursed himself for being naïve. There would be very little time for all those altruistic ideas he had been filled with just a few moments earlier, indeed rather than feeling like he was the decision maker, he now felt out of control.

He called in his first patient. Rudyard Kipling came to mind *"if you can keep your head . . ."*, but he only had a short interval between his somewhat nervous initiation with the intercom system which had resulted in a barely intelligible airport style effect in the waiting room, and the patient arriving at his room, yet in that pregnant pause a message flashed up on his computer screen.

"Whatever you do, don't laugh" was the message. He read this just as the lady entered his room. Now he knew for a fact that this patient was a lady as the name suggested it and the notes confirmed it. However, he was forced to choke down an involuntary splutter of amazement and (ashamedly) amusement as he was right now confronted with the most marvellous full black beard. He quickly chastised his tea for going down the wrong way, resisted the devilish voice in his head saying "tell her it was a hair ball", and turned back to his hirsute patient. Now this was not just some naughty extraneous lip hair that could be waxed out of the way intermittently. No, this was a well groomed, full on beard. Greg found himself desperate to look anywhere else, but found that his gaze was drawn magnetically back to fix firmly on the magnificence of the beard. The patient never batted an eyelid (not that

Greg would have noticed), and launched directly into her agenda. She even seemed to be rather proud of her follicular state.

Fortunately for Greg she was only there for a routine review and to get some more medication, so he was able to gather himself, recover some semblance of poise, and do the necessary, before she left and he was able to take a moment to get himself together.

He replied to his warning message explaining how he had almost choked on his tea, then spilt half over his desk, and within moments—seemingly too quick for a kettle to boil—he was furnished with a steaming fresh cup. All in the name of experience he thought, and at least he had gotten the comedy consultation out of the way for the day.

He called in his next patient. A rather stocky but malodorous man fairly stormed into the room, bearing a shaved head, various facial scars looking suspiciously like knife wounds, and multiple tattoos. He just about managed to arrest his momentum without actually ramming into Greg, panting in his exertion directly into Greg's face. There had clearly been very little attention given to dental hygiene over the past, well, entire life really, leaving the rotting stench of end stage tooth decay lingering in the air. Rather worryingly he was sat directly between Greg and the door, and even seated seemed to tower over everything in the room. He was hunched forward with knuckles clenched on thighs, like a crazed pit bull waiting for the slightest excuse to be unleashed in all its fury. There was a small respite for Greg, since sentence construction was not high on his list of abilities, giving him time to make sure he was calm and didn't say anything inflammatory. He most definitely did not want to antagonise this character.

He noticed from the records that the patient had not been seen at the surgery for the past two years, and then it became evident why this was the case. A spell at Her Majesty's pleasure had precluded any visits anywhere for a while. Including the dentist. The intimidating appearance was not aided by the fact that he shouted everything. He shouted at Greg that he had just gotten out of prison, and had just come in to get his sick note.

When Greg then referred to the notes to see what had occurred during the last consultation, he saw that a sick note had indeed been issued two years ago, just prior to the period of incarceration. However, the note had been given for an ankle sprain, for the period of two weeks. Greg was a little confused. He decided to ask the patient what his current medical problem was that required a sick note today.

"For my ankle" he shouted back.

Greg was now in a sticky situation. He attempted to explain to his intimidating patient that a sprained ankle could reasonably be expected to take around four to six weeks to heal, and that there should really be no lasting problems relating to such a sprain, and that unfortunately it would be neither possible nor appropriate to issue a further sick note now two years after he had actually sprained the ankle itself.

It took some time for this to slowly sink in, and for the patient to digest its meaning, during which Greg was rapidly becoming increasingly fearful for his own personal safety. When it finally registered, a look of pure rage descended on his already challenging face, then he stood up towering over Greg, and threw his chair across the room, shouting

"You're wots forcing me back into crime"

He clenched his fists in a reflex reaction, revealing tattoos across the knuckles which read 'love' on the left, and 'hat' on the right (his right little finger was missing, presumably Greg supposed, from some previous altercation where he had probably punched someone so hard it had simply fallen off from the shock of the impact).

"You fucking wanker" he continued; all the worse for being spoken at a volume similar to that of a rock concert. He then stormed out of the room, much to Greg's relief, leaving him physically unharmed, but distinctly shaken. He didn't think he really deserved such a tirade for refusing to continue a sick note two years after a simple ankle sprain, and felt it was perhaps a little unfair to suggest that he was the reason that the patient might decide to undertake further criminal activity. Heaven forbid he actually take any responsibility for his own actions, and indeed his life. No, the taxpayer had obviously not supported this character enough to date, and it was rather unfair to expect him to actually work.

Only two patients seen in his first surgery, and already Greg was feeling like an emotional wreck. His head was spinning, and his body was charged with adrenaline due to the behaviour of the last patient. He was distinctly on edge. Unbeknownst to him though, his next patient on the list had just seen the last one leave, and had decided to take it upon themselves, along with her four sisters, to head straight round to the consulting room without waiting for an invitation. Ordinarily this would not have been a problem, but in Greg's current state of nervous frailty their silent, almost stealthy appearance around the corner took Greg completely off guard. His nerves were already shot, and so the appearance of the five sisters caused him to actually cry out in fright. He genuinely thought for a moment that he was being attacked by a group of ninjas, and jumped out of his seat to the back of the room.

He later reasoned that if this had in any way offended the group of women in full black burkas, then they only had themselves to blame for sneaking up on him in the first place.

Once he had realised their benign nature, settled himself, and sat back down they were able to begin the actual consultation. The problem was that they all proceeded to talk at the same time, which was all the more confusing since he could not see their mouths. They all talked on behalf of the one sister who was apparently in "too much pain". Greg was very tempted to ask them what they would deem to be the correct level of pain, but managed to resist. He heard "too much pain" repeated at least eight times over the course of the next few minutes, leading him to assume that the patient was indeed in some pain, and would therefore warrant an examination. Then she refused to let him examine her.

"But you are in too much pain" he said without a hint of sarcasm

"yes"

"and you would like me to find out why, and presumably try to get rid of this pain"

"yes"

"but you're not going to let me examine you"

"no"

"did you ask to see a female doctor?"

"no"

"did you know I was a male doctor?"

"yes"

"so you knew that you would not let me examine you"

"yes"

"did you think I could work miracles?"

"I am in too much pain"

"but I cannot tell you why unless I examine you"

"I am in too much pain"

"so am I"

Greg was fully aware that his frustration was beginning to show, and was not proud of it, but what on earth was he supposed to do? He felt impotent. His only course of action was to eject all five of them out of the room and send them back to reception so that they could book their sister in with a doctor whom they would allow to examine her. With any luck they would then be able to ensure that she was left with just the right amount of pain.

The years of training, of honing skills, acquiring knowledge, the pressures, the stress, all for this shit! His list continued to grow before his eyes, in a seemingly never ending chain of misery, if his first three patients were anything to go by. Unfortunately for Greg it didn't really get any better.

At medical school it had been drummed in that 90% of diagnoses could be made from the history alone. Great care and attention was given to developing history taking skills, since it was such a vital part of being a doctor. However, the whole premise rested on the fact that you were able to actually communicate with the patient. The rest of Greg's morning consisted of patients from such a wide variety of countries, it was mind boggling. He saw Slovakians, Latvians, Poles, Somalians, Angolans, Kurds, and many more, none of whom could converse in English. There were no interpreters available, due to various spurious reasons from the trust such as they cost too much or we don't really care as long as they are registered somewhere. It all became rather veterinary, with hand signals, gesticulations and a great deal of frustration. It also took a great deal more time to try and work out what the problem was when you were unable to just ask. How was he supposed to give medical care to people with whom he could not communicate?

At times he was able to utilise a telephone interpreter service when it was available (sporadically), but struggled to understand the person on the other end of the phone, complicated further by the long delays resulting from their location in a distant continent. They in turn had no idea how the NHS worked, which meant trying to briefly explain the system before even beginning to attempt a pseudo-consultation.

On top of all this, there were very few actual medical issues to deal with once he had worked out why they were there. He had a request for a letter to enable the patient to get a better house, another requesting a better job, another requesting a sick note for two weeks for a "holiday" (that one took some explaining ie. That's not quite how the benefits system works here etc, etc), and various requests for letters to solicitors regarding immigration cases. Not a disease process in sight! A pathological desert. He felt like screaming out at the waiting room

"I'm a doctor; show me someone who is actually sick! Show me someone I can actually treat! Even someone I can talk to would be a start!"

He finished his surgery with patient number twenty eight of the morning, by which time he was utterly emotionally drained. She was an elderly lady who spent the first ten minutes explaining at great length how much she adored Dr. Dulcis, and oh, how lovely and kind and caring he was. He insisted that she always come to see himself and no-one else, and he would always have time for her, and make her feel special. She told Greg how she always brought him a nice bottle of wine, just as a token of how grateful she was for his kind attention. Of course she didn't have one with her today as she could only manage to get an appointment with Dr. Finn, a most displeasing scenario, about which she would be having words with the practice manager.

She didn't really think that Dr. Finn ought to change anything at all, since Dr. Dulcis knew all about her, and he might not like it, and she would come back anyway next week (and indeed had already booked another appointment to do so) no matter what Dr. Finn said, so that she could be sure everything was OK with Dr. Dulcis.

"It's nothing urgent anyway" she explained as she gathered her handbag, gloves, phone, keys, hat, scarf, shopping bag and coat, and gradually made her way towards the door, all the time explaining to Greg how much she was looking forward to seeing her hero again next week. It did beg the question "why the fuck did you bother coming in the first place?" which Greg bravely whispered indignantly once she was well out of range.

Her exit did signal the end of his first morning surgery, and precipitated a huge sigh of relief. If this was how it was going to be, then he was quite worried. As he was already late he decided to make his way directly to the doctors meeting room, where they would all gather at the end of each morning surgery, and was looking forward to a coffee, a sit down, and a supportive chat with his new partners.

The room where the doctors would congregate was rather pretentiously called the 'conference room'. Greg opened the door and walked in with a little trepidation after his morning of unexpected intensity. The doctors were sat in luxurious brown leather armchairs around a large coffee table talking with the practice manager, presumably having a conference. There were overflowing pigeon holes on the wall on one side, and the holiday calendar on another, already marked out for the next twelve months. Outside it was raining.

The manager, Debbie, was somehow perched arrow straight on one of the reclining chairs, looking quite incongruous with the relaxed nature of the furniture. She looked as though her vertebral column was made of steel, a meerkat sentry watching out for danger, or perhaps she was maintaining tension to make sure her love eggs didn't fall out in public. She certainly was smiling anyway. But when Greg looked more closely, it was more of a wide eyed fixed way too bright smile. Like an air hostess dealing with a bunch of loud mouthed drunken idiots, whilst trying to maintain the professional smile. It was almost a grimace. Her demeanour and personality seemed to match her appearance, being remarkably robotic in nature. Alongside her neat suit, and close cropped neat hair, came an almost hysterically cheery voice, which immediately grated on the nerves, especially nerves which had seen quite enough for one day thank you very much.

"Good morning Greg, have you enjoyed your first surgery?" she asked with a loud optimism, totally lacking in sincerity.

They all turned towards him, noticing his presence in the room for the first time.

Greg's initial thought was that she might well be taking the piss. She couldn't possibly be serious could she? What kind of new super human level of ignorance was required to think that he could on any basis have enjoyed that? Witty comebacks began to rattle through his mind as a natural reaction to such a question, but it was clear that she had meant it. She must have. She didn't possess the wit to have even a semblance of a sense of humour.

They were all still staring at him. He decided that since it was his first day he would reign in and respond with a non-committal

"yeh, it was fine thanks." To be fair that was really all that the facile question deserved.

"Great!" she replied. "I bet it's just nice to know you're working in the best practice there is?" she said this with utter conviction, without hint of sarcasm or irony, and waited expectantly for Greg's impending complimentary reply. The doctors showed no sign that this was comical. Indeed they all looked at him expectantly themselves, and Greg was sure he heard a "here, here" from somewhere in the room.

"Er, yeh" was all he could manage from his state of shock at having landed in some other dimension where everyone was a total cock.

His response seemed to appease them for the time being, and Greg was just relieved that he hadn't burst out laughing at their immense pomposity. Debbie herself turned away in a very precise fashion back to some paperwork that she had brought with her for the partners perusal, still smiling maniacally. Of course, paperwork was like porn to her. She almost drooled with pleasure like an expectant spaniel.

She appeared to have the happy disposition to be extremely pleased with herself all of the time. Greg had an unusually strong urge to punch her in the face. Instead, his attention was required by the four partners who were now addressing him with their condescension. His new colleagues. There proceeded a kind of pseudo-welcome from the most senior partner, Dr. Simon Superbus.

It was some way into the speech that Greg noticed that the senior partner was actually standing up, since he still only reached the same height as the other seated partners, and in fact well below one of the others. He was vertically challenged to the extent that his stethoscope which was still hanging from his neck, was almost dragging on the floor, looking a little like a leash. This was not an altogether inappropriate thought since he was renowned to have a rotweiler of a personality, and was fortunate in his ability to be able to continue to look down on people from the grand heights of around five feet up.

He did, however, make up for a lack of height with an excess of width, giving him an essentially spherical appearance. The source of this width was fairly apparent in the alcoholic ruddy glow of his cheeks. If you tried, you could almost smell the hops pervading through his skin and clothes. To complete the picture, he sported a head shaved to disguise the recession of grey hair, and clothes so worn they really ought to have been consigned to the scrap heap many moons previously. Surely he could afford to buy a new shirt occasionally, rather than persisting with a once white now grey with deodorant stains under the arms monstrosity. He had disguised his short man syndrome effectively at the interview, where he had seemed charming, but his robust, dogmatic reality was now very much evident. The welcome speech was perfunctory, and in no way improved Greg's impression of his first day in the practice. It was essentially now you're here, get on with it.

Dr. Geoff Dulcis was a different kettle of fish altogether. He was friendly and chatty, bordering on intrusive. No, actually, when Greg thought about it he was just plain bloody nosey. He was someone whom you could instantly warm to, only later to realise that there had been an altogether different agenda on his part. The trouble was he had bright blue eyes and a cheeky boyish smile, which meant he could get away with asking you things that others could not. Pretty soon you would be lured into answering inappropriate questions as if he had just enquired as to the time of day. In fact, within a few minutes he had already found out that Greg was not gay (his first question, but in a cheeky boyish fashion), was married, and no his wife did not do anal. He had been caught like a small mammal in the gaze of a cobra. He later found out that if, for some reason, you had a burning need to know which of the staff had tattoos and where, then he would be able to tell you. If you then had a further burning need to know which of the staff had a Brazilian, a Hollywood, a Bollywood, a Las Vegas or a Californian, then again he would know. There was a kind of dedication there, even if it was disturbing in nature. How many employers knew the pubic styling of each and every one of their staff?

This reminded Greg of an urban myth at medical school, where a gynaecological procedure was being performed on a lesbian woman who had died her pubic hair green, and sported a tattoo across her lower abdomen which read "keep off the grass". The surgeon had to shave the area for hygienic reasons, and so took his marker pen and wrote across her abdomen for her to read when she awoke from the anaesthetic "sorry, had to mow the lawn!"

Dr. Dulcis ran late. Always. It was not medical thoroughness that made him run late of course, more his penchant for knowing personal detail. He selected his own home visit and left the conference room to continue with his surgery, since he was only around half way through. The trouble was, in order to make up for the exponentially increasing time his patients had to wait to see him, he had to give them exponentially more time in the consultation, and more general pleasantness and chit chat, which of course they expected next time, so making him late again, and so on and so forth. He was an appeaser. As long as everyone still thought he was a bloody nice chap, then all was well.

Dr. Morag Asper talked a lot, and very loudly, in a harsh and grating timbre with a mild Scottish accent which became stronger in relation to her level of anger. This explained why she mostly spoke with an extremely strong Scottish accent.

She didn't even register a flicker of recognition regarding Greg, as though he simply did not exist. She had a typically Celtic complexion, with short straw coloured hair, and a cold, mean face. Even seated she was clearly excessively tall and painfully thin, with gangly limbs desperately trying to conceal themselves behind one another. Greg thought her attitude was unashamedly rude and had no choice but to sit through her lambasting all those unfortunate enough to be within earshot (which encompassed quite some distance) about how awful her morning had been, how unfair it all was (life presumably) and how this was just typical and always happened to her. His ears rang with her indignation, as she could find no other option other than to storm out of the room in sheer frustration at how harshly life was treating her, forgetting, of course, to take her fair share of the home visits.

Her exit was in stark contrast to that of Dr. Superbus, since she must have been at least seven feet tall, with all the femininity of a scrotum, looking remarkably like a giraffe with haemorrhoids. Greg realised that if he had to look at that in the mirror each day, then he too might conclude that life was pretty unfair.

Dr. Hilary Rudis remained at the table, in conversation with Debbie. Greg thought that she could most kindly be described as frumpy. She seemed to have a most unfortunate habit of reclining back in the armchair and resting both feet up on the coffee table. This would be fine if she didn't also place her feet quite some distance apart on the table. This also might not be so bad if she was wearing trousers, but no, she wore a skirt. Just as with the bearded lady of his morning surgery, it was simply impossible not to look at the flabby, cellulitic white thighs laid open for display. Would it be inappropriate for him to mention such inappropriateness on this his first day? His optic nerves were already reeling from the freakish nature of his morning, and were in danger of being permanently damaged by the toxic image which confronted him. Optic neuropathy caused by intense disgust. It took all his willpower not to stare, and instead focus on what she was saying. It was clear that the only opinion that mattered in the world to Dr. Rudis was her own. She had a politician's ability to refuse all manner of rational intelligent argument, and continue in blissful ignorance of her own self importance. She was plain in appearance, but wore paradoxically bright and colourful jewellery, and reminded Greg of those dog lovers who dress their canine obsessions in clothes and jewels. It just seemed wrong.

She explained the distribution of the home visits for the day. Dr. Superbus had taken old Mr. Thomas, as he apparently knew him very well indeed, and so it was appropriate for him to go. The comment as to the reason for the visit itself was "a sticky eye". The address was two doors down the road from the surgery. In essence, the entire visit would, therefore, take all of five minutes to complete—a fortuitous co-incidence?

Dr. Dulcis always went to visit Mrs. Templeton, who baked a fresh cake for him whenever he went round. She was fortunate to be favoured with home visits on a much more frequent basis than most patients.

Dr. Asper clearly wasn't doing a visit that day since the world was so unfair to her, and none of her partners were going to dare dispute that. They knew from experience that they would receive one of two reactions. Either a screaming tirade or tears. Both were perfectly honed to ensure that no visit would ensue, having been used to great effect many times before.

Dr. Rudis had decided that she was going to see Mr. Simpkin and his "sore toe" as he lived conveniently on her way home for lunch. Her tone made it clear that this was not up for discussion.

That left Greg with Mrs. Coulton, who was apparently "off it". As he perused the map to find out where Mrs. Coulton lived, it became clear why she had been left for him. She lived beyond the furthest reaches of the practice boundary, a relic from many years previously when the catchment area had been much greater.

During the forty five minute drive through the city traffic, Greg had a flashback to when he had read the practice profile before his interview, confidently declaring the "scrupulously fair and democratic" approach of the doctors, and wondered whose arsehole they had pulled that one out of.

Had they only survived by each creating their own method for dealing with the hellish nature of the work? The volume, the intensity, the sheer bizarreness, the sense of futility, the sense of it being a conveyor belt, all leading to various versions of anger, rudeness, self importance and self protection. Or were they already like that anyway? What would he do? Would he find his own method, and if so would he too become as objectionable as they all were, and if he did would he realise it?

The prospect of becoming anything like what he had just experienced in the conference room was so abhorrent he was feeling quite nauseated, as he crawled along, wipers at full tilt, heading for the next instalment of his ever worsening first day.

Greg pulled up outside the terraced house, in an area of the city which had once been a friendly community. The older residents who had been there for some time had suffered to watch the inexorable deterioration as the area had steadily been overtaken by benefit cheats, crime and drugs. Now the few remaining decent folk were afraid to leave their homes.

He walked up to the door, noticing the presence of an old mattress in the front garden, and various bits of rubbish dumped for convenience. He was about to grasp the door handle and head directly inside (as he had been instructed when Mrs. Coulton requested the visit) when he just about managed to stop himself in the nick of time. He inspected the handle more closely and was able to confirm that yes, it was indeed smeared with shit. His training allowed him to deduce further that this was human shit.

"What the fuck am I doing here?" he muttered to himself, and wondered if judging by the exterior, the interior would also be a cess pit. He managed to root around in his medical bag and find some gloves which he donned before reaching again for the door. He wished he had covers for his shoes, a face mask, and an oxygen supply, took a deep breath and went inside.

The front room was gloomy and dank. There was a distinctive aroma that you would usually associate with public toilets, but here it seemed to suit this home. The curtains were drawn except for a slither of daylight which served only to highlight the smoke filled dusty room. There was the debris of self neglect littered all around the place, and there were multiple other smears of faeces daubed randomly over carpet and furniture. All this unfolded for Greg as his eyes became more accustomed to the semi-darkness.

Finally he realised that his patient was also present. Against the far wall, perched in an armchair, sat an elderly and frail looking lady. She was staring blankly in his general direction, and the effect along with the surroundings was a little unnerving.

"Hello Mrs. Coulton, I'm Dr. Finn"

"I hate doctors" she replied in a sort of half controlled screech.

"I see. Well, you did ask for us to come to see you, so how can I help?"

"It's my chest."

"And what is the problem with your chest?"

"You're the bloody doctor"

"OK, well, what symptoms do you have?"

"It's bad"

Greg struggled on valiantly for a little longer but remained impressed by how little she would reveal to him about how she was feeling. It was like she was deliberately making it harder for him. Let's see how good a doctor you are shall we? You can have minimal to no information and see if you get it right. He hadn't exactly hit the heights of a textbook doctor patient relationship, but he was beginning to get used to the feeling. And it wasn't for lack of effort on his part.

He resolved to move in closer, aiming to get to within touching distance, determined to win her over, but as he did so he noticed several things all at the same time.

First of all, there was the most disturbing sensation beneath his feet. The carpet was becoming increasingly sticky the closer he came, and he began to feel worried that his shoes might actually stick solid. He understood the problem, but the understanding in no way helped his mood. The ever increasing concentration of human effluent the nearer he came towards its source was the obvious culprit. He had never seen anything like it in his life. Here he was standing in a dark smoky room, in a sticky mess of human piss and shit, directly in front of a woman who hated him, and was doing all she could to prevent him doing what he had come to do, which was to make her feel better.

The second thing that he noticed on having moved closer was the appearance of two strange piles, one on either arm of her chair. On the right was a pile of cigarette ash. In some ways it was a remarkable model of physics. It was all balanced in such a perfect way such that not a single further atom of ash could be added. This didn't stop her trying though, and as she did, Greg observed the unsuccessful ash tumble down off the pyramid towards the carpet below where it then dissolved amidst the urine soaked fabric.

On the left arm was a similarly well balanced pyramid, this time formed by used tea bags. Again several unsuccessful tea bags lay seeping into the carpet to the side of the chair, having failed to cling on.

Greg was aware that he was facing a situation which seemed, inexplicably, to have escaped his medical school teaching sessions. He cursed his tutors for their lack of foresight, and tried desperately to think what to do. He was disturbed to note a strong urge to simply write out a prescription for some antibiotics and get out of this hell as quickly as possible. He was disturbed by its appearance in the first place, but he quickly dismissed the idea as it was just not him. He always hated hearing stories about how badly his friends, colleagues and family had been treated in general practice, and couldn't help taking it personally. In fact, almost as soon as anyone knew what he did for a living, they started to tell of their own horror story at their doctor's surgery. He was never sure quite what they expected him to do. It did make him angry though, especially hearing about doctors handing out antibiotics without even examining the patient, and here he was, day one, with that very idea appearing in his head.

However, it's not necessarily the ideas that come into your head, rather how you respond to them that matters. So Greg gingerly leaned forward to examine Mrs. Coulton, taking excessive care to avoid the various obstacles in his path, and making a mental note to thoroughly sterilise all his equipment the moment he returned to the surgery.

She had a chest infection after all, and so he proceeded to write out a prescription for antibiotics. When he later looked back over events, he had no idea why he then did what he did, but sometimes words just tumble out of your mouth before you really realise what you are saying. For some unfathomable altruistic reason he decided to tackle the issue of hygiene and self neglect. The torrent of foul abuse surprised even him, and was still ringing in his ears as he lunged out into the fresh air, having narrowly avoided various missiles thrown in his direction, most of them tea bags.

Some people just don't want to be helped. Perhaps it was patronising to think that she did. She obviously must be aware of the state she was in, since she was perfectly alert. But then that was his job wasn't it? Not to be patronising, but to try and help. All she had wanted was some antibiotics, then for him to piss off with minimum fuss. Bloody doctors.

Greg had made his way back through the traffic just in time to enter his visit onto the computer, take a deep breath and be ready to start the afternoon surgery. He still felt stressed from what had passed so far, and had not had time for any lunch. He was now into his siege mentality, and was fixed on just getting through it and getting home.

The afternoon list was a further twenty patients, with a continuation of the morning's theme, with several patients again with whom it was simply not possible to communicate. One family came from a small village in rural Somalia, and spoke their own language that was only known in their locality. Greg had no hope. The man looked about seventy, and his wife about seventeen. More hand gestures, mimes and some guess work.

There was a succession of people suffering from stress, most of whom seemed to have much less stressful lives than his own felt at that moment, and lots of depression. He was feeling pretty depressed himself. He was pretty sure it wasn't contagious, but he began to wonder. Add in a couple of personality disorders, a few alcoholics, and several heroine addicts, and the afternoon was progressing nicely.

He was becoming proficient in recognising and dealing with the habitual request which came with every single consultation with an addict for something, be it sleeping tablets, pain killers, or indeed anything that could be flogged on the black market to pay for the next hit. Some of the sob stories were really quite inventive. He was targeted disproportionately as the new doctor, the thinking being that he would be an easy target, but they seemed unaware that he had all their records in front of him, including those from the specialist drug unit, telling him exactly what they should and should not be taking. He began to take some twisted pleasure from feigning empathy when they told him they had gone without their sleeping tablets. He would look concerned and ask how long for, and how terrible it must have been, to which they would reply that it had been over a week doctor, and how awful it was, aiming for maximum effect, maximum sympathy, and hence the best chance of a prescription. At this point he would brighten up and explain to them that if they had gone a whole week without them they were no longer addicted and no longer needed them at all, so well done! Then would proceed a silence while they tried to think of some way around this, couldn't, and left.

Finally he was ready to call in his very last patient of the day. He steeled himself, and hoped for some real medicine, a chance to utilise his skills, something to salvage what appeared to be the job from hell, something inspirational, where he could really make a difference.

In walked a twenty three year old male, recently moved down from Newcastle, in a very forthright fashion, and sat down in the chair. Greg smiled and asked

"How can I help you?"

"I've had a headache every single day for the last two years. I've seen doctor after doctor and no-ones dun nuthin. You have got to do something to sort this out right now."

As the patient was speaking, Greg's mind was racing through possible differential diagnoses. Young male, persistent headache, what do I need to ask, do, examine. I will sort this out for him, I must. Think.

"Did anything to seem to start it all off at all?"

Good Greg, open question, gives the patient a chance to elaborate, gives time to observe, assess, and evaluate where to go next.

"Yeh, when I shot myself in the head"

In retrospect he thought he probably shouldn't have laughed out loud. No, he definitely shouldn't, but in the face of such provocation he was simply unable to stop himself. The patient stood up and walked out looking unimpressed by yet another unsatisfactory consultation. Judging by this reaction, Greg thought he had probably received similar medical feedback before. He was also able to notice as he left that there was a large depression in the frontal area of his skull consistent with a bullet exit wound.

When Dr. Dulcis was consulted by the same patient several days later, he had already been briefed by Greg, and so was able to avoid laughing, and find out some more information. He had indeed placed a gun under his chin and pulled the trigger. He had failed with the intended suicide, but on the plus side he had managed to cure himself of the depression which had driven him to attempt to kill himself, by performing a DIY lobotomy. Indeed he could no longer recall having ever felt depressed in his life; even when he had shot himself in the head.

As it was now nearly seven o'clock, and he was faced with a half hour drive home, he thought he would call his wife and let her know he was on his way. It had been an unexpectedly horrendous start to his new job, and so a sympathetic ear and a kind word were just what he needed. They were just what he needed but not what he got. How thoughtless it was for him to have stayed at work so late. He never did anything for her. Not interested in the trials of his first day, she was keen to berate him with how difficult it was for her to organise hair appointments, beauty treatments, and on top of all that, deal with her mother.

She was a true expert at guilt (a catholic background ensured this) and was seemingly always able to make it sound like she was the victim. Greg placated, apologised, and sped òff through the early evening traffic amidst a plethora of emotions. He decided that he definitely did hate his new job, but it was only day one and things might improve. However, his instinct kept reminding him that it was the antithesis of what he wanted.

He then had to try and manage the mixture of emotions his wife provoked. He felt guilty for being late, and responsible for her current and perpetual miserable nature. It was up to him to "cure" her of this, and ensure her permanent blissful happiness. However, it seemed the more he tried to do so, the more effort he put into doing things for her, the more thoughtful he tried to be, the more she complained of being miserable. Maybe it would be better when his first pay slip came through, enabling her to ease her misery through the medicinal use of plastic.

But then he also resented her misery. He felt used, taken for granted. Her misery and the threat of it prevented him from doing the things he wanted to do for himself.

He certainly did not feel loved, which ultimately was what most people wanted more than anything else. As he arrived home he had decided once again to opt for appeasement. An offer of dinner at a smart restaurant had a remarkably swift beneficial effect on Mrs. Finn's constitution.

If he was truly honest with himself, he never felt quite comfortable in such establishments, but it was just what his peer group tended to do, and so he went along with it. He found it distasteful to spend that much money on a meal, defeating the object really. He seemed to have a social conscience, but one that lacked the conviction to actually change behaviour, just enough to make him feel bad.

He loathed the looks on the faces of fellow diners. The "what are you doing here? You don't belong in such a fine restaurant, alongside the likes of us. How selfish of you to ruin our evening by your impertinent proximity."

The whispered conversation, the clinking of cutlery, the frowns that would greet any hint of laughter, the exorbitant price of wine, and the condescension when it came to ordering some. How he would usually end up ordering the second least expensive bottle on the wine list so that it didn't look like he had just gone for the cheapest.

Then there were the frequent interruptions to any already whispered conversation, as the waiter returns repeatedly to top up your wine for you (which you couldn't possibly be trusted to manage by yourself), and then your water, and then your wine again after you made the mistake of taking a sip. So you have to stop your whisperings every time the waiter appears, fragmenting any dialogue even further, since you couldn't possibly let them overhear your oh so important conversation, or more likely how banal it was.

He was sat surrounded by self important pricks, feeling thoroughly on edge, with the knowledge that he would have to pay a small fortune for the privilege. Anyway, if it kept Mrs. Finn bordering on content for the evening then it would be worth it.

Once they had decided (i.e. Mrs. Finn) that they had had sufficient, there then followed an uncomfortable ten minutes or so for Greg in desperate search of a waiter from whom to request the bill. They had been annoyingly ever-present whilst they had been eating, hence when they were not actually needed, but had now vanished.

It was impossible to try and continue a conversation as he had to repeatedly swivel around in his chair in the hope of catching sight of someone to resolve this awkward scenario. Mrs. Finn looked at Greg with resigned disdain, a look which she had perfected over some time, and was clear in its intent to make Greg feel as though it was all his fault.

This made Greg feel like it probably was all his fault, which in turn allowed an unavoidable guilt to creep in. He then felt guilty about allowing himself to feel guilty about something which he knew really was not actually his fault.

This was typical for how time spent alone with his wife would proceed. A seemingly endless turmoil of negative emotions, constantly eating away at any chance of contentment.

Eventually a waiter made a brief appearance some distance away. Like an animal used to being hunted, only a brief timid glimpse was offered before disappearing again to the safety of the "staff only" haven. But Greg's vigilance paid off, and his meerkat like surveillance allowed him to convey his message instantaneously during the brief glimpse that was available, using the well known mime for "bill please" utilised by all seasoned restaurant goers. He had seen his father do the same, and others too, but whenever he mimed writing across his palm he couldn't help but feel like a twat. He was sure the waiter thought the very same. Nevertheless, the bill duly arrived.

The bill itself really ought to have had its own fanfare. Due to its magnitude, he felt obliged to scrutinise it to ensure fair play, and found a use for his experience at trying to decipher medical notes in various but unanimously appalling handwriting.

Greg noted at the bottom of the bill that theyhadthoughtfullyaddeda"discretionary" tip of 12.5%, and that this entry was all but illegible. Presumably this was in the hope that most people wouldn't notice, and add a tip themselves based on the bottom line. This made Greg really quite angry. Firstly, the presumption that the meal and the service would be worth an extra 12.5%, and secondly the poorly disguised attempt to wangle even more out of people. The more he thought about it, the more he began to seethe. His underlying mood did not help. However, not being one to make a scene he decided to seethe in silence.

It still took him some resolve to refuse to leave an additional tip on top of the tip, and struggled to look directly at the waiter who collected the bill, even though he had consented to their own idea of a tip.

"I hate these fucking places" he thought to himself. He only came because of her. He was sure he sensed people staring as they left the restaurant, and he just wanted to get out, get home, and go to bed.

He was feeling guilty in the taxi about the damn bill, and then he felt guilty about letting himself feel guilty again over another thing which was not his fault.

However, he had at least achieved the intended goal of placating Mrs. Finn's ire enough to see them through the evening without receiving too much additional persecution, largely through the double edged sword of fine wine. She was happy (well as close as it was possible for her to come to such an emotion) looking blankly out of the taxi window, occasionally sniggering at the homeless littering the pavements at that time of night.

"What a day" thought Greg. He knew he was looking at a disturbed night's sleep, having spent a small fortune just to eat some food, in the necessary appeasement of his wife, due to the fact that he had had a nightmare of a first day in his new job. A job he didn't even want in the first place.

He was concerned he might actually be going mad, medically, technically, but there was no way on earth he could let Mrs. Finn think he was anything other than absolutely fine with everything. Goodness knows what would happen if he did. No, he would continue to hide his unhappiness; keep up the appearance.

Having arrived home, they went straight upstairs to bed, each having their own routine which kept them well out of touching distance of one another. They slept in a bed that would comfortably accommodate a small village, ensuring that they never had to actually come into physical contact. They could text each other goodnight (out of politeness), and if either wished to read for a while, the other would not be disturbed by only being on the very edge of the glow from the distant bedside lamp.

Mrs. Finn was fully dressed as usual for sleep, including face mask and ear plugs. They didn't have sex. At all. It was virtually impossible for Mrs. Finn to reach and maintain the perfect level of inebriation which was just enough to bring about the required sexual disinhibition, but not so much that she fell unconscious. Such a dream combination had only been achieved twice during their entire marriage.

Greg wanted sex; in fact he was pretty fucking desperate. It was there all the time nagging away at him. Tumbleweed blew through the intimacy vacuum of their massive bed, with Mrs. Finn fully clothed, snug and snoring away at one end, and Greg at the other, lying naked as always, discontented, frustrated, quietly seething again, wondering what was wrong with him.

Having come nowhere near to any sort of decent preparation for a good night's sleep, he spent a troubled night with various thoughts buzzing around in his head. It was like his mind had put itself onto spin cycle just when he wanted it to be silent. He knew he needed to get some sleep before having to get up for work the next day, so he tried to force relaxation.

"I must relax. I must relax. Why aren't I relaxing? Come on, damn it, relax!"

He thought of so many ways to try to clear his mind that it was alert with the very ideas themselves. For all his efforts, he was the antithesis of calm.

Eventually, he gave up even trying to fall asleep, and soon afterwards, he fell asleep. Unfortunately, as soon as he had drifted into the much needed deliciousness of deep and restful slumber, his alarm went off.

He physically dragged himself up and out of bed, feeling as unrefreshed as it was possible to be, and tried to contemplate the prospect of another day at the Narcissus Group hell hole. He couldn't help but resent the loudly snoring form of his wife lying undisturbed, while he groped his way out of the room and downstairs, where he couldn't face breakfast, and so just left.

He was soon part of the chain of traffic, gradually making ground towards the city. Endless cars, people, tarmac, concrete, buildings, lights, road works, all for the privilege of another day of shit. Then it would start again but in the other direction once the day was over, gradually gaining ground back towards a house, chores, the television, then bed, then start it all again.

It was time for "thought for the day" on the radio. Given his current mood he thought he might actually listen to it for a change, and see what gem of spiritual wisdom was on offer to inspire him for what was sure to be a difficult day ahead. It was a mark of how low he was feeling that he had forgotten how listening to this part of the morning radio programme had always made him feel in the past, and why he was now used to just turning it off until it had finished.

He listened to a female vicar enthusing about "God's plan" which had apparently been responsible for "all of creation" and then managed to relay this to the important events of recent news. This didn't seem like a very good thought at all in Greg's view. In fact it seemed more like an anti-thought. Hadn't she heard of evolution? Everywhere you turned these days, be it the radio, the news, television programmes, documentaries, magazines, newspapers, the internet, and anywhere else, people always had to talk about the evidence. Evidence for or against this or that and definitely the other. People make decisions about so many things on a day to day basis influenced by evidence. So why, Greg wondered, was evidence not discussed when it came to religious ideas?

You had to be so careful not to offend someone's beliefs, but people didn't seem to mind so much when it came to something like scientology, and even less for those firmly committed to living as Jedi knights, but as far as Greg was concerned there was no more evidence for one over the other. It didn't seem to work the other way either in Greg's experience, finding fervent followers of any major religion to be frequently offensive if you refused to toe the line, switch off your brain, and follow what they told you blindly without question.

Two women had come to his home not long previously, asking if they could read some sections from the Bible to him. He politely refused. One of the women told him that she knew an atheist, and even he liked to read from the Bible, and actually he was quite a nice man. Greg had been astounded at the time. It was clearly a remarkable occurrence that someone could be an atheist and a nice man at the same time; that you could be a decent, moral, good person without having to be told how to do it. Greg responded by informing the lady that he knew a Christian who was also quite intelligent. She didn't seem to get the point.

Greg thought you would have to be pretty deluded to not accept the evidence for evolution, but then you would have to be pretty deluded to believe in an omnipotent all seeing creator sitting somewhere up there in the ether (sorry, heaven) listening in to our every thought, judging our every action, waiting to dole out some form of petty punishment whenever we stray from "His" way. That seemed to be quite judgmental didn't it? And what about the billions of people who have ever lived believing in other religions? Were they all just plain wrong? Were they all, in their immense majority of billions immediately banished to hell for all eternity because they believed something else, because their family had believed it, and their families before that? It didn't seem to make any sense at all to Greg. He just couldn't imagine that if there was some higher power that it would behave like that. Just then he ran into a traffic jam.

Our first thought on encountering a traffic jam probably ought to be something towards hoping that there were no major casualties from the pile up ahead, and that no lives had been ruined by a momentary lack of concentration, such as reaching forward to desperately try and turn off "thought for the day". Instead the usual reaction is more "why me", "why now", or "I'm going to be late for work".

The delay gave Greg some further time to explore his thoughts on religion. Essentially, he surmised, it was all down to ego. The ego doesn't feel particularly great about the fact that death is inevitable. It gets pretty annoyed by this actually. It can't accept that it is a natural part of life itself; the conclusion which has to come. It doesn't want to contemplate its own demise, the loss of its possessions, its knowledge, its achievements, its status. All those things that the ego wants to cling onto will be lost. So being really very annoyed by this prospect, it has to come up with some kind of escape route to convince itself that this can all be avoided. Hence life after death, and some form of deity.

Given human nature, and how even religious people in the past have been proven to be less than perfect in a moral sense, their egos then think "I can get some mileage out of this one", and so organised religions appear, allowing particular egos to prosper even more, and take advantage of all those other egos just struggling to avoid the contemplation of their own demise.

When he thought about it further, it seemed pretty egocentric to think that some great and almighty being, some immense and vast intelligence, would give a toss about what he was thinking or doing twenty four hours a day, never mind every other person who had ever lived on the planet.

"He can obviously manage on less sleep than me" muttered Greg. Then what about all the animals? Was there a moral code for zebras? Do the ones with bad thoughts get eaten first? Like if they ate the wrong bit of grass, or had an urge to mate with some other stallion's mare, the lions are tipped off, and that's it, curtains for you evil zebra. Are the gates of Heaven barred for particularly lustful aardvarks? We share so much DNA with other mammals, and have common ancestors not very far back in the scheme of things, that he felt he was not being entirely irreverent.

The traffic began to merge and flow more steadily, and presently the cause of the delay was revealed. A rather angry bald fellow in a pin stripe suit was shouting and gesticulating into a mobile phone. He was quite overweight, causing rolls of himself to bulge out past the restraining capacity of the suit, and his anger ensured that his face steamed in a remarkably vibrant red.

His Porsche lay unmoved, unmoving, despite the tirade. This cheered Greg immensely. He thought of a new slot for the morning radio:—"Schadenfreude for the day". Yes, he thought, much more inspiring.

The girls behind reception seemed mildly surprised that he had even turned up for another day. They were delighted to receive a cheery morning greeting, being unaware just how much effort it had taken on only his second day, and he breezed through to his room to find a steaming cup of tea ready and waiting for him. This small act again filled him with at least some energy and even hope; mainly that things couldn't possibly be as bad as the previous day surely.

He considered his own attitude, and wondered whether a different approach might work better for him. But then he would not be true to himself, but then there was little point being true to yourself if it led you to a breakdown was there? But if he did then he could not stay here and then what would he do?

He recalled different approaches taken by people in the past, and particularly recalled Professor Bentham, infamous consultant ear, nose and throat surgeon at medical school. He was especially frightening to students, partly due to his status, but largely due to his eccentricity. Greg had been present when he had made one of Greg's fellow medical students climb inside a cupboard in his clinic room, before proceeding to call in an actual patient for a consultation.

Greg recalled how he sat there aghast as the professor began the consultation as if there was nothing going on at all, until there was an opportunity to let the patient know that

"I've got a medical student in that cupboard"

He then proceeded to examine the patient as if this was perfectly normal. The patient himself looked somewhat confused, and not surprisingly was unsure what the correct response to this comment should be. He settled for staying quiet and endured the ear probing in silence.

"Come out Carter" called the professor. To the great surprise of the patient, a medical student did indeed at that moment emerge from the cupboard right on cue.

Greg's biggest problem was in stifling laughter which, if noticed, would ensure he would be picked on next. The humiliation was not over for poor Carter though, as he was then bombarded with questions that he was never likely to know the answers to, even if he was not already flustered from having just emerged from a cupboard.

Of course, the questions were deliberately too difficult, which ensured incorrect or absent response, allowing the professor an excuse to take out from behind his desk a rather large inflatable hammer which he wielded with altogether too much enjoyment, repeatedly hitting Carter over the head for each wrong answer.

It was probably less important to develop a lasting doctor patient relationship in ear nose and throat surgery than in general practice, but Greg felt that such an approach was perhaps a little extreme and might come across as somewhat unprofessional. It was not quite textbook consultation skills. In fact he couldn't imagine what on earth the poor patient must have thought, but he was pretty sure he would not be filled with trust, confidence or respect.

No, Greg reckoned he would have to find some compromise. If he was to survive he would need to evolve, but he could not let himself become as dismissive or cynical as the professor and in any case he didn't have a medical student handy.

As is often the case when expecting the worst, that morning he was blessed with some charming and amazing people, usually of a certain age, most of whom had come through great adversity without complaint and were still able to remain polite, generous and considerate.

They warmed quickly to Greg's underlying easy going nature, and he regretted not having the time to listen more. Unfortunately the pressure of appointments and the time it took for the necessary examination of several rectums got in the way of extended conversation.

One elderly gentleman explained to Greg mid examination, that he was fortunate, as this was only the second time in his life that another man had touched his bottom and the first one had gotten a "bunch of fives".

What was just another routine part of his job for Greg, a clinical emotion-free procedure, was something entirely different for a patient. It was so easy to become blasé about what you were doing, and its effect on the person in front of you.

This was rammed home (perhaps not the best choice of phrase) very clearly when he had to perform the exact same examination on another gentleman that same morning. He explained clearly what he was going to do, in a kindly manner, and did his best to have the patient at ease and comfortable. He said his usual

"A little cold gel . . . now take slow deep breaths" before inserting his finger (gloved) and starting his routine for the examination.

"Bloody hell doctor, it doesn't half put you off being gay!"

This response took Greg off guard, and he could not stop himself cracking up. The trouble was that as a result of attempting to stifle the laughter, he began to shake with the effort, which caused his arm to shake, and hence also the still inserted finger. He grabbed his arm to try and steady it whilst he got himself under control, hoping he had not caused some sort of vibrator like effect.

The gentleman left after the consultation, leaving Greg pondering what had been said. Greg wondered what the thought processes had been. Had he said to himself

"Hmm, since I have the chance, I think I will see how it feels to have something shoved up my rectum, and if I like it I might even go and bat for the other team for a while. After all, I've liked girls for long enough, so maybe it is time for a change." Is that how it works?

Greg concluded his morning surgery in a much better frame of mind, with a sense that he had made some positive difference to at least one or two people today. He had, of course, also helped an elderly gentleman confirm his own heterosexuality.

He emerged from his room and passed through into the back office for a dose of mild sexual harassment from the girls. He had already noted how Sandra had a habit of nudging her bosom and strutting around looking way too much like a drag act, leading the rest of the girls in a gifted deluge of innuendos, which suggested much previous practice.

The trouble was that Greg had never really been confident amongst the opposite sex, and blushed easily when he found himself in the unwanted position of being the centre of immediate attention. They were like a wolf pack sensing a weakness. At the first hint of a blush they almost howled with delight and pursued him relentlessly, making him blush even more, like at the scent of blood, sending them into an innuendo frenzy. You could hear Sandra's ovaries bouncing around her pelvis by the time Greg was able to escape whimpering to the conference room.

When he arrived with a sigh of relief, though secretly he had enjoyed the attention, he found the room deserted. When he examined the visits book, he found that the other doctors had seemingly managed to finish remarkably early, and had already chosen their visits and left. It also seemed that all the local visits had been taken, somewhat conveniently, leaving co-incidentally, the one that was some distance away for Greg.

The only other information was a note reminding everyone that there was to be a meeting at lunchtime, and that sandwiches would be provided. Greg noted the reason for the home visit request, which was "abdominal pain" (which could mean virtually anything), and that the patient was in his seventies and had only recently joined the surgery, so there was no previous history available for him.

He had plenty of time on the long journey out to the patient's home to moan to himself about how he would no doubt miss all the best sandwiches, and would be left with egg and cress on wholemeal cardboard, and wondered how he might approach the issue of fairness when deciding which home visit they all took.

He was greeted by a relative of the patient, and ushered through the living room where a vast crowd of other relatives were anxiously waiting. He was a little intimidated by the number, and a little worried by their expressions—like he was their shining hope.

The patient was upstairs, so he went directly, unable to shake off the idea that they were waiting for some sort of magic trick. The patient was clearly in some discomfort. Greg introduced himself, and spoke kindly and gently, and laid his hand over the offending abdomen directly whilst he continued to talk.

Greg's own heart raced as he felt the large pulsating mass beneath his hand. He knew immediately the nature of the problem, and how very close to a swift death the patient now teetered. He calmly reached for the telephone which lay on the bedside table and dialled 999, promising to fully explain once the ambulance was on its way. He then had to break it to the patient that his aorta was on the point of rupture. He did not move until the paramedics arrived only moments later to escort the patient with all haste directly to the vascular surgical team whom Greg had also alerted, and who were waiting, ready, in the emergency department. It was all up to them now. He spent some time explaining to the massed relatives downstairs what was going on, trying to find the right balance between giving some hope but also preparing for the worst.

He later discovered that the patient had suffered a cardiac arrest just as he arrived at hospital, but that since he was absolutely in the very best place at that moment, they were able to resuscitate him well enough to take him into theatre and repair the leaking aorta, and save his life. It had all been touch and go throughout.

Greg shivered at the thought that had he lingered a little longer that morning, had he stayed for a chat, for a coffee, had he been stuck in some traffic, any of which would have meant him arriving five minutes later at the patient's house, then that man would now be dead. Had he taken his time trying to work out what was going on, taken more history, talked more to the relatives, then that man would be dead. That multitude of people who clearly loved the patient would now all be grieving. Instead he had acted quickly, decisively and correctly, and had been one link in a vital chain, each of which were essential; him, the paramedics, the emergency staff and the surgical team. The NHS working at its very best. He felt an overwhelming humility, bordering on a sense of panic at the responsibility. How amazing it was that all those skilful people had come together to save a life. He had just been the beginning, but nevertheless not many people get to go home at the end of the day knowing that they had helped to save a man's life. Perhaps the job wasn't so bad after all.

Greg entered the conference room and sat down in one of the leather chairs with a rejuvenated and heightened awareness that not even the lack of taste of egg or cress on wholemeal cardboard could diminish. And so the meeting began.

The meeting itself was regarding the complaints that the practice had received over the past year, which was necessary as a contractual obligation. Greg had managed to make it through a day and a half without generating a complaint, so he was able to just watch and listen with interest as to how his partners handled the proceedings. He wondered how he would feel, and imagined it would create some difficult emotions, and he would probably feel quite defensive.

There was a list of complaints to discuss, and so the chair person Dr. Asper began by making it aggressively clear that the sooner they got this irritating tick box exercise over and done with the better, and that they should all avoid procrastination and just get on with it. They could then write the whole thing up in the most disingenuous way to make it look like that they had actually taken it seriously if anyone bothered to ask. The whole attitude of the meeting was to imply that Narcissus was the best practice in the city, so any complaints from whatever source must be either unfounded or mad.

Greg soon found out that this wasn't altogether untrue, when they turned their attention to the first formal written complaint on the agenda. This concerned all the doctors, and was a complaint about why they all refused to prescribe this 76 year old lady hormone replacement therapy.

In her letter she dismissed the concerns regarding the associated risks for someone of her age as "rubbish" and proceeded to explain that she had absolutely no concerns about the risk of breast cancer anyway, since she always checked herself whilst she was masturbating.

The image in Greg's mind at that point was seriously disturbing. A sexually charged septuagenarian, lustfully rubbing her bosom, stopping for a moment to note "ah, no breast cancer" before continuing on to reach a successful climax. The combination of sexual urge meets health check seemed very odd. He couldn't imagine a bloke cracking one off whilst checking his testicles for lumps at the same time. But then that was multi-tasking and blokes were not supposed to be able to do that anyway. Maybe she was just being efficient. The complaint, having been "fully discussed" was filed in a folder marked MAD.

There were several complaints regarding Dr. Dulcis which surprised Greg given how much the patients loved him, until he noted the reasons which were all regarding access. Time after time it was how they couldn't get in, or didn't have long enough with their favourite, how were they expected to survive without their weekly review, and repeated emotional pleas via tear soaked hand written letters.

It genuinely saddened Greg to witness such false dependence, and unfortunately he knew Dr. Dulcis colluded. It was his reward back, to feel so needed. Why?

The rest of the complaints were mainly to do with the attitude of the doctors, and were mostly concerning Dr. Rudis.

"She didn't listen"

"She was rude"

"She fobbed me off"

"She never looked at me, just the computer and her watch"

Like water off a duck's back, these were smoothly and seamlessly dealt with en masse with admirable efficiency and minimal of fuss, to such an extent that even Dr. Asper's usually granite face betrayed a moderate softening, since that meant the end of the complaints. Dr. Rudis had given those complainants all the attention she felt they had deserved, leaving them all free to congratulate themselves on how open, self-critical and reflective they had been.

They also felt the need to comment that it was a shame that other practices in the area (and for that matter the entire county) couldn't accept constructive criticism like they could, learn from it, make any necessary changes, and so aspire to drive themselves up somewhere near to their own standards.

The practice manager was told to make sure that the outcome of the meeting was published in the practice newsletter so that the patients could feel satisfied that their concerns had been thoroughly addressed. They then proceeded to disperse towards their own rooms amidst a great big delusion of altruistic fervour, Dr. Asper stooping down to get through the doorway, and Dr. Superbus going through sideways, leaving Greg still sitting down utterly stunned by the whole process.

The theme for the afternoon surgery was bad skin. Greg felt he was justified in questioning why, if you knew you were going to see a doctor regarding some whiffy appendage, couldn't it be washed first? Why did this never seem to be the case? One patient's state of personal hygiene was so utterly devoid of attention it had managed to create a halo of offensiveness with no small radius all around him, to such an extent that it was causing significant distress to anyone unfortunate enough to cross its path. Several people had collapsed in its wake, and there appeared a strangely high incidence of depression in the surgery that afternoon. These were found to be cases of reactive depression, secondary to severe stench, cured not by antidepressants so much as a nose clip. As a consequence, and purely as a public health measure, Dr. Finn felt he had no other option other than to admit the patient for, as his referral letter stated, "a damn good wash".

Two whole cans of air freshener, and a great deal of wafting, and indeed waiting, were required to return the consultation room back to a state fit for purpose. The enforced twenty minute break to fumigate the contaminated no go area of his consultation room allowed Greg time to step outside, fill his lungs with not so clear city air, and the nauseated sensation to disperse, enabling him to return feeling just about ready for the next patient.

Having taken such extreme measures to ensure a tolerable environment, Greg was absolutely livid at being able to smell the next patient coming before he had even set eyes on him. A middle aged, greasy haired, acne scarred man in a long trailing black leather jacket appeared through the door. He had made it easy for himself to find his way back out of the surgery by leaving a trail of flaked off skin behind on the carpet, like string through a maze. His route had been somewhat tortuous, probably thanks to his impressive level of inebriation. A broad Liverpudlian accent announced cheerily

"Hiya mate!"

"I'm not your fucking mate" whispered Greg to himself, resenting the further assault to his already besieged senses, all the time fighting to remain professional. The patient didn't see the irony in Greg's next question

"What seems to be the problem?"

"Well actually doc, it's my, er, skin."

"No shit."

When he subsequently disrobed, a veritable shower of flaking skin drifted to the floor, looking a little like a light covering of snow.

"Oh, for fuck's sake" thought Greg. He was faced with some sort of apparition from a science fiction or horror film, with layer after layer of cracked and flaking skin, oozing and weeping with pus which seeped from various points on the torso. Matters were at their absolute worst in the region of the groin which emanated a stench the like of which, if harnessed, could be used as a chemical weapon. The ultimate deterrent.

Greg spent a great deal of time sorting out the best treatments for the patient, to de-scale, cleanse, moisturise and generally disinfect, and arranged for him to return at the end of the week to see how it was all going. In fact he felt like he had done a pretty thorough job, especially given the circumstances. The patient seemed pleased, and had left to follow his skin trail circuitously back to the outside world.

After a further bout of fumigation and some judicious vacuuming, Greg was able to complete his surgery and finish what had been another intense and eventful day at work. He put some Crowded House on the car stereo and tried to imagine he was driving through rolling green countryside rather than through the industrial estate, but his mind wandered back to his home visit. It could all so easily have had such a different outcome. That man's life, so frail, so vulnerable, so precious, so random. He supposed that was why he was forced to pay a small fortune every month to a legal defence company. He wasn't allowed to work unless he was covered against potential litigation, and the buck stopped with him around fifty times every day, hence the risk, hence the cost. Thinking about it provoked a minor panic attack. Anyone who wasn't suitably scared by it all ought not to be doing the job in the first place he thought. Over confidence was not a good trait in a doctor, and in Greg's experience always led to disaster. For some reason his thoughts turned to his new partners.

Greg arrived home to the news that six of Mrs. Finn's acquaintances were coming round for dinner, and were due to arrive within the next thirty minutes. Whilst he was musing to himself about the potential reaction which would ensue if it was the other way around and he had invited friends round for dinner and informed his wife at the last minute, he was also aware that this was, as always, a double edged sword. On the down side he was annoyed and frustrated about not having been informed, and what this said about how his wife treated him, but he also knew that it would fall to him to produce a three course meal at the drop of a hat. She didn't do cooking. Greg liked to cook but mainly when he had time and when he was prepared, being somewhat of a perfectionist. That had been his mistake; to actually produce some half decent meals, effectively ensuring he ended up doing most of the cooking.

On the up side, however, there was the diluting effect of company to help ease the passing of the evening. He was able to descend into his own reverie, knowing from experience that they wouldn't be interested in anything he had to say anyway, and confident that conversation would not be directed towards him, allowing him to blank all else out, focus, and achieve some bizarre sense of inner calm.

The way they scraped their plates clean as though they hadn't eaten for a week told him at least that it had been edible, even enjoyable. Nevertheless a thank you would have been nice. He volunteered, alone, to clear the table and wash up, and so avoid further conversation that he would not be involved in anyway. With such distraction around, he was able to retire in peace to read his book and go to sleep.

The rest of his week progressed in much the same insanely busy and emotionally draining manner as it had begun. It was brutally clear that this was the norm. This was how it was going to be as a partner in this surgery for the rest of his career. The thought of staying there for the long term was incredibly depressing. The thought of morphing into some sort of despicable clone of his other partners was even worse. He could not imagine how they could have such blinkered, distorted, bastardised opinions of themselves, their role and their patients. Had they always been like that, or had they evolved over years in the job, and if so would that happen to him like it or not if he were to stay. Granted it was a good salary, but surely there was more to life and work than earning money. Maybe it was just early days he thought to himself but he knew that this was a delusion. It was really very clear to him that it would never, could never improve.

The trouble was he desperately wanted to be liked, to be good, to be thorough, and he did also actually care. He was so frustrated by the lack of time to devote to the genuine people who were in real need, the ones who of course would never want to bother him even though they were the ones who ought to the most. They were swamped by the absolute deluge of hypochondriacal, malingering time wasters who fully expected him to sort out their meaningless existences no matter how long it took, and were incapable of ever understanding that they were not actually the centre of the universe.

When he had a moment to reflect, a brief interlude amidst the madness, he saw it all for what it was. It seemed like every other patient was morbidly obese. It seemed that the ever widening societal gap between rich and poor, those that have and those that don't, was mirrored in an ever widening gap between the thin and the fat. This began to irritate. He spent so much time listening to complaints of backache, knee pain, sore feet, breathlessness etc, etc, but if he ever dared to suggest that there might perhaps be some connection to their gargantuan size, that perhaps the human skeleton was not adequately designed to support the weight of a medium sized whale, then of course great offence would be taken.

"I only eat a lettuce leaf a month doctor I'll have you know."

"And I run at least a marathon every day."

"I'm always active."

"I never stop."

Yeah, never stop eating Greg thought. The level of denial was incredible. Perhaps there was indeed a medical explanation for this. Perhaps over a certain weight it became inevitable for globules of fat to coalesce around the brain and squeeze it to a point where it was unable to function, where it could no longer see the blindingly obvious.

Greg was worried he was becoming a little obsessed. He was finding morbid obesity to be obscene, almost immoral, certainly distasteful (if only they did too). Every week on the news there were stories about less fortunate people having to deal with severe food shortage, hunger, starvation, malnourishment, and death. People, children, were starving to death, and Greg was having to spend time dealing with lists of health problems essentially caused by eating too much.

Such thoughts made him feel guilty. It was not in his nature to be judgmental but here he was thinking all of this. They were human beings too, no less worthy of the very best health care than anyone else. Or were they? There were already restrictions made based on how much alcohol a person drank, or what drugs they took, or whether they smoked. Was it so different for people who refused to stop shoving cake down their throats?

He decided to write a weight loss book. He planned it all out roughly on a piece of paper filched out of the printer. It was very clear, easy to follow, and if applied correctly was absolutely guaranteed to bring about serious weight loss, and so rid the country of this growing public health epidemic. It went as follows

Page 1: eat less

Page 2: exercise more

Page 3: stop lying

Page 4: the end

He realised that the simplistic brilliance of this method would most likely go unrecognised, largely since it involved some actual effort on behalf of the patient. He had found in his experience that ironically most people preferred their weight loss to be handed to them on a plate. A very large plate with a side order of chips.

This was by no means the only idea swirling around in his brain. He considered havingthesupermarketsputalltheunhealthy food down the same isles, protected by a trapdoor at either end which gave way at a certain weight, or have the isle sides so close to each other that they simply could not get down. But then he thought that they would just persuade a thin person to shop for them. Like teenagers outside a newsagent, furtively approaching those allowed in with

"get us a pack of sausage rolls mate"

No, those ideas would not work. Then he wondered about the option of being able to prescribe six months in rural Sudan for those of greatest mass. It didn't have to be specific, other countries could join the programme as long as they had a long term shortage of food and no processed or fast food options available.

An enforced holiday from anything processed, from crisps, biscuits, cakes, chips, pizza, microwaves, television remote controls, televisions, cars, the internet and mobile phones really ought to do the trick. Somewhere it was just not possible to sit around on your arse all day. They could even be enrolled in some form of humanitarian project, thereby helping themselves and others at the same time. Genius, surely?

Greg was beginning to worry that this job was making him a little too cynical. Was he becoming someone full of anger, resentment, losing his compassion amidst this mass of bullshit? Was he more irritable with himself (how the fuck should I know?).

Richard Johns

He had been on the very brink of screaming at an unfortunate Kurdish man with whom he consulted via the aid of a telephone interpreter. There had been the usual scenario of seemingly immense soliloquies which then miraculously translated into one word answers, eventually revealing that he had only just arrived from Iraq (where he had lived all his life at around 40 degrees in the desert). He had arrived in the cold and damp of an English winter, and after some time Greg was eventually able to extract the reason for his attendance to see the doctor that day, which was the revelation that he

"Felt cold"

Greg was concerned that he was missing something. He asked the interpreter if he was sure that this was the problem, if there were any other symptoms, if he could have misinterpreted his meaning. A rapid fire five minute long conversation then followed, back and forth, eventually leading to the interpreter concluding to Greg that yes he was indeed sure that the problem was that he felt cold.

Greg asked the interpreter to explain that it was minus five degrees outside, snow lay on the ground, he felt cold himself, everyone felt cold and considering this chap had just arrived from Iraq he would be concerned if he didn't feel bloody freezing.

The interpreter kindly managed to explain this to the patient in what seemed to Greg to be a solitary word. The patient seemed to understand, and left to buy a hat and some gloves.

His increasing irritability showed itself again when he consulted a frail lady in her eighties, about which he later felt somewhat ashamed. She had been patient number 21 out of 30 for the morning, and he was already stressed by the impossibilities of time management. She took the entire allotted appointment time just to shuffle around the corner of the corridor from the waiting room.

Greg was frustrated, that was his excuse. The moment she rounded the corner, carefully placing the Zimmer frame out in front of herself time and time again but achingly slowly, and then saw him at the door waiting for her, she began to talk. She barely stopped for breath. Greg was genuinely concerned she might not take the time to oxygenate herself out of a much more pressing need to get it all out, and that she might actually turn blue. At least she would match her hair.

She talked as if this was her one chance in her week. A willing ear that was unable to flee out of the door. She had given him most of her life story by the time she made it to the actual consultation room, and having gleaned that she had come mainly for a repeat prescription and a natter, he surmised that were she to sit down she might never leave. He decided to simply set her into an orbital rotation, printed off the desired prescription, and was able to hand it to her as she came around full circle to face the door again. He was then able to set her directly on her way back down the corridor and off to the waiting room.

After all his efforts earlier in the week, he was surprised when flaky skin man failed to show up for his review appointment. Whilst a result in an olfactory sense (and others too), he was nevertheless disappointed that he had obviously failed to engage. He could at least look back on that home visit as something positive to take out of the week, though there was little else.

It was the weekend, and Greg had the pleasure of being the doctor on call for the practice, meaning an emergency surgery Saturday and Sunday mornings. This was frustrating since he really wanted a lie in, and even more so since he knew that Mrs. Finn had a long list of chores for him to do once he had finished his surgery. There would be little chance for any time to wind down, and the prospect made him grumpy.

It felt strange driving in to the city to work at the weekend. There was none of the usual traffic, and the city itself had a strange eerily empty feel as he made his way through the streets. They lacked their usual hustle and bustle, the sense of purpose and activity of the working week.

At the surgery, there was only himself and two members of staff, so the atmosphere was calm and quiet. No throngs of people waiting at reception, getting angry, frustrated, and increasingly loud in expressing their displeasure at something or other.

There were no routine appointments, just emergencies on the day itself, and he found that his morning was mainly concerned with dealing with mildly ill children, whose parents were the ones who were really in need of the consultation. There was not, however, the pressure of appointments, so the pace was much more pleasant, helped along by several cups of tea.

Then along came a "management consultant" who "managed" to park his oversized Mercedes across most of the car park, including the section marked with large yellow paint saying "do not park, emergency vehicles only". Of course this area was closest to the front door for obvious reasons, so despite the fact that the entire rest of the car park was virtually empty, he obviously felt he shouldn't have to walk an extra few yards, completely ignoring the blatantly obvious but mildly inconvenient.

He proceeded to stroll in to the surgery in a very executive fashion, in a manner which suggested that it was a privilege for the practice to be blessed with his presence; especially on a Saturday. He arrived in his own time into Greg's room, and explained that he had been having a particular problem for a month or two, and that he was now fed up with it, and that Greg ought to sort it out for him, pretty much this instant really.

He was sporting a brightly coloured jumper with a designer label, flashed his similarly designer pink socks ostentatiously, and loudly clattered his Mercedes keys next to his Blackberry on Greg's desk. Was this all done to try and impress upon the doctor how important he thought he was; to clearly mark his social class territory, or was it all done without any agenda just because he was an arse?

Greg explained that just as he had been informed by the staff when he rang to make the appointment, this was an emergency surgery, and that perhaps if he had had a problem for a couple of months he could have come in earlier.

"Well, I'm an important man. My time is limited, what with work, and of course golf" he replied in a supercilious manner.

"We do have appointments from seven in the morning, and also until around seven in the evening, which are there for people who have difficulty fitting their health care into their busy lives."

"My boss will simply not allow time out in the week, so I'm afraid it's just not possible"

Greg wanted to say something to the effect of it being highly unlikely for there to be any detrimental consequences from you not being present at some meeting spent entirely discussing when and where the next meeting would take place, or sipping endless coffees twiddling expensive pens trying desperately to feign some level of intelligence, whilst checking out your secretaries legs, until finally the vacuum between your ears eventually recognises the one thing it is capable of which is that it is at last time to fuck off home, allowing your ego to then congratulate itself on a fine day of business at the office.

"So what is this problem then?" he settled for instead.

"Well I've been feeling quite tired"

"As medical emergencies go, that's not exactly up there"

"Well it is according to my osteopath" he replied.

"What?"

"I've seen an osteopath privately, who diagnosed a misalignment in my spine which he was sure was the likely cause. He spent quite a few sessions putting everything back into the correct place again, but since it hasn't really changed my symptoms at all, he suggested that there must be something seriously wrong with my energy lines, and that I ought to see a doctor as a matter of urgency. So I booked an emergency appointment."

"When did you last see him?"

"A week last Thursday"

"Hmm. What made you see an osteopath in the first place may I ask?"

"My reflexologist recommended him. Once I explained this to my boss, he let me out of a few meetings and paid the fees for the consultations, he is very supportive that way."

"So why won't he let you come and see a doctor?"

"He doesn't like doctors"

"Is it in case we actually find something wrong perhaps? Never mind, you were saying that your reflexologist recommended an osteopath"

"Yes. Well, she thought it was really unusual that her own therapeutic interventions had not resolved my problems, and so she thought I had better see someone else to try a different approach."

"And did these therapeutic interventions consist of rubbing your feet?"

"Well, largely, yes."

"And you're surprised that neither this, nor manipulating your spine has cured your tiredness?"

"Well, yes of course."

Greg wondered how such a self proclaimed successful supposed intelligent business person could be so stupid. He decided to deal with the issue since he had no other patients waiting, and so took a detailed history. He asked about his lifestyle, diet, sleep pattern, work, and anything else that might possibly affect matters, and then performed a thorough examination. He found two very large nasal polyps, one in each nostril, which were responsible for the loud snoring which had been annoying his wife so much, which had led to some major arguments, which had led to her leaving him and moving back to stay with her mother for the past month or two. This had in turn led to him drinking half a bottle of single malt whisky every night, which combined with the nasal polyps meant an extremely disjointed and unrefreshing nights sleep. This made him feel tired.

Greg carefully explained the findings and the relevant issues, and gave him some treatment to try and help reduce the size of the polyps, but also referred him to see an ear nose and throat surgeon to see if they ought to be removed. If he could also remove the malt whisky ritual, then he might start to sleep better again. Perhaps then he might be able to resolve matters with his wife.

"I see" said the patient, and then paused as if reflecting hard on something. "But what about my energy lines?"

"Perhaps we can address them once you have managed to get some sleep"

"Very well doctor. What should I say to my reflexologist and my osteopath?"

Greg considered replying with "have you considered a medical degree—they are quite useful if you want to work out what's wrong with people?" Instead he settled for "how about thank you for all your help, but I won't be needing to see you anymore?"

Saturday's emergencies having been dealt with, he headed home to make a start on his chores. He walked into the house to find Mrs. Finn in a characteristically foul mood. She had only recently risen from slumber, but despite it now being the afternoon, unfortunately remained "fucking knackered".

It seemed that the only sensible and indeed reasonable way to proceed, therefore, was retail therapy, with the added incentive of allowing Greg to get on with his chores in peace. There was a very clear expectation that today's list would be completed by her return, otherwise a confrontation would ensue the like of which would make Attila the Hun cling to his teddy bear weeping for mercy. And then she left for the shops. Greg didn't have a teddy bear, so he sat on the stairs and wept a little to himself.

Sunday morning surgeries were usually quiet. Greg wondered why this was the case. People clearly had much better things to do on a Sunday than have a medical emergency, and who could blame them. The last thing Greg would want to do if he could at all help it would be to have to go and see a doctor, particularly on a day where you were supposed to be able to relax and enjoy yourself.

The prospect of a lovely lie in, doing some activity you enjoyed, or spending the day with the family all probably explained why there were so fewer perceived emergencies on a Sunday. Greg wasn't complaining, since he enjoyed the enforced peace. He found it rather like his most favourite time to be at work, whether whilst working in hospital or during his time so far in general practice, which was without doubt when England were playing football. This was simply the best time to be at work as a doctor.

Greg didn't care much for football, finding it really quite boring. On occasion when he had been forced to sit through entire games he just got irritated by the players throwing themselves onto the ground when anyone came within a six mile radius. This was usually during some international competition where England were expected to win, having been convinced this was the case by the blind faith of the supporters, pundits and journalists without having considered the fact that the other teams in the competition all had much better players. They would then proceed to fall at some early hurdle before returning home to feel the pain in their million pound mansions and on their extended summer holiday in the Caribbean.

However, he couldn't deny that football was immensely popular, to the point of fanaticism. This then had an effect on the health service. An as yet undiscovered law of physics must be implicated at such times as an England football match, leading to some kind of pathological black hole, since nobody ever needed to see a doctor when a game was in progress. If only they could be more like cricket test matches and go on for five days.

Perhaps Greg had missed the concept entirely, and should become a little more broad minded in his assessment of football and its effects. Perhaps it was the ultimate panacea. Perhaps more football ought to be screened, and more widely. Perhaps a large screen could be placed in the surgery car park, allowing people to make their intended visit to the doctor, remain in the car park, watch a game, then simply go home afterwards feeling very much better or at least having forgotten why they went in the first place amidst the non-medical fever of post match analysis. They wouldn't even have to expose themselves to all the germs floating around the waiting room, or bump into people they didn't want to see, or undergo any embarrassing or uncomfortable examinations.

Greg realised he hadn't really thought it all through. What about all the counsellors, psychotherapists and psychiatrists? They would be left with very little to do. Just place a large group in a room, put the footy on and leave them to it, and ninety minutes later out they come having forgotten their problems, in deep discussion over a penalty decision. They could always re-train as additional pundits, since they would be needing many more if this were to be rolled out nationwide.

Greg thought he had better be careful to keep such thoughts to himself, and not mention these amusing wanderings which his brain decided independently to pursue at any opportunity, especially anywhere near anyone from the Department of Health, since they were genuinely likely to put it forward as the next major development to transform the NHS for the better. You could never underestimate the idiocy of those making policy for the health service.

This Sunday was typical, in that it was very quiet. Greg was able to spend some time catching up on the paperwork which had amassed during the week, and had dictated letters, reviewed notes, and filled in a variety of insurance forms, and was feeling pretty good at having cleared his desk. He had settled down to read New Scientist to pass the time until the end of the allotted surgery hours, and was enjoying the calm.

Then there was a gentle knock on the door.

"Come in" said Greg, wondering who it could be.

In walked Emma, one of the reception staff, but she was not working that day, and as a result caught him off guard since he had never seen her in anything other than the extremely unflattering and poorly fitting uniform they were forced to wear. Why was it so strange to see someone out of the context that we are used to? Greg was repeatedly amused when politely greeting patients he knew when he bumped into them outside of work, say in the supermarket. They would say something like

"Oh, I didn't recognise you without your glasses"

Greg found this odd; I wear glasses sometimes, and lenses other times, but they are definitely not magic spectacles; they don't change my facial features, they are just a simple pair of glasses, how can you possibly not recognise me? Anyway here he was flummoxed by seeing a member of staff in clothes other than he was used to seeing her in; and she never wore glasses.

She closed the door before moving in a feline manner over to the chair next to Greg. He observed her open toed high heels, revealing bright red painted toenails, skinny jeans and a tight fitted top, her long dark unrestrained hair and her radiant, if a little concerned looking face.

Her perfume hit him like a sledgehammer in the pelvis, to such an extent that she was forced to repeat what she had just said to him since he missed every word in a state of complete intoxication.

He mumbled a reply, saying that no, of course he didn't mind her coming to ask his advice. His mind had turned to mush. A spinning vortex of emotions and feelings.

She was sensational. She made him feel like an adoring drooling puppy. How easily it had happened; he was meant to be the professional, and it took some serious force of will to gain a semblance of control, and to bring his mind back from the status of primeval goo to being a highly trained and intelligent diagnostic tool again. Having just about gained back some conscious control over his power of speech, he was able to encourage her to explain the problem.

She had apparently gone over on her ankle whilst in town, and wasn't sure whether she ought to go to casualty but quite reasonably didn't want to suffer the four hour wait if it wasn't necessary, and would he mind having a look to see how bad it was?

Greg tried to speak as little as possible, as when he did he sounded like he was on helium, and proceeded to examine her ankle; and what an ankle! He found he needed to keep himself bent forward to disguise his inner primal stirrings which would do little to aid the appearance of professionalism.

He was reminded of his friend Robbie from medical school who had invented the syndrome of inappropriate erection, or S.I.E. This had been in the context of having to stand for hours in operating theatres assisting the surgeon, surrounded by various theatre staff (mainly female) dressed in surgical greens, which gave little protection when the inevitable appeared. The problem was that it seemed to become an ever increasing issue. The more you tried not to think about it, to stop it happening, to think about anything else, to focus entirely on the patient's internal organs and the procedure you were assisting, the more it seemed to happen. It was always there ready to leap out at you at the slightest chance.

The other issue was timing. It seemed much more likely to happen when it would perfectly coincide with a break in proceedings. This then meant you having to feign some sort of stomach cramp, and hurry bent over past the nurses and theatre department assistants towards the nearest lavatory until it eventually subsided, lulling you into a false sense of security only to reappear as soon as you returned to a public area. When you knew what you were looking for, you found that it was actually much more common than you might initially think.

Male medical students would be witnessed dashing to and fro across the theatre department corridors desperately seeking the nearest empty facility, bent forward, doubled over, cringing, occasionally nodding to each other with knowing looks

"S.I.E.?"

"Oh, yeah!"

Greg had not suffered a relapse for some time but here he was in the middle of a severe flare up. He kept himself pulled up tight against the desk, hiding his shame, and repeatedly sent silent messages to himself saying "go away, go away", whilst attempting to explain to Emma that she had a sprain of her ankle ligament and that casualty was not necessary.

She smiled back at him in a fashion that was of absolutely no help to his predicament. He began to fear that his desk may soon show signs of levitation when she finally released him from the torture and left, having thanked him for being so kind and helpful. She told him that it wasn't difficult to see why the patients had warmed to him so quickly, and why they already asked to see him in particular. No, it wasn't hard at all, was it, she murmured with a twinkle in her eye, before walking out of the room taking her cat like figure with her.

Greg took some deep breaths "in and out, in and out; no, that's not helping, just breathe", and felt like he had just completed a morning of dangerous sports. His heart was racing, and he had an adrenaline high. His flare up of that syndrome gradually faded as the clock moved forwards to the end of the surgery and he was free to go home.

On his way back he suddenly pulled the car over outside a pub, having recognised one of the punters standing outside with a pint of Guinness and a cigarette on the go. It was flaky skin man. He was most surprised to be accosted by Dr. Finn on a Sunday, and promised to come and see him for that review.

Greg whistled and smiled his way through his chores for the rest of the afternoon, which did not please Mrs. Finn who found it distinctly unreasonable for anyone to be so unnecessarily happy.

Monday morning was strangely a much brighter prospect and Greg found it quite unnerving that he was actually looking forward to getting in to work that day. He spotted Emma amidst the crowded back office immediately, noting that she had covered over the shapeless uniform tent with a small black fitted cardigan which was much more suited to showcasing her figure. She was getting on with her usual reception duties, only she somehow managed to do so in what seemed to Greg to be an incredibly sexy fashion.

The rest of the girls were also busy as usual, but stopped for a moment to inform Greg excitedly of an impending night out at the weekend, and would he like to come along. Of course his correct response was that he would have to check with Mrs. Finn, but he was going to make damn sure that he would be there.

When he made it round to the conference room to check his pigeon hole, he found Dr. Superbus was already there having a cup of tea and conversing quite loudly with himself. He even managed to talk down to himself Greg was amused to note and cheered up at the entrance of Greg as an audience for his ramblings.

He delighted in informing Greg of the details regarding how he had managed to send "the wife" on a shopping spree, allowing himself the freedom to tour round some of the local public houses. Of course it was essential to relay how frequently he was recognised in each of the establishments, which was clearly the desired outcome, aiding the quite unnecessary boosting of his already ample ego.

Dr. Dulcis duly arrived, and proceeded to converse with Dr. Superbus about how miserable his wife was and how he had so many bloody chores to do. Greg had an awful premonition that this could be him in ten years time. A rapidly greying ruddy cheeked remnant of what used to be a decent looking bright eyed young bloke, sporting an impressive middle aged spread, who was much more content when at work than when at home in the company of his wife.

Surely this had to be wrong. It seemed so sad. He could not, must not let himself get to that state. Dr. Rudis appeared gulping down her third coffee of the day in the manner of a heroin addict desperate for a hit. She was utterly incapable of managing anything other than a primeval grunt until enough caffeine had suffused into her system. We are talking about enough to make a bull elephant jittery. Unfortunately for her patients, this was pretty much impossible to achieve much before around four o'clock in the afternoon, rendering her communication skills for the most part on a level with a less than averagely vocal blancmange.

Dr. Asper completed the morning pre-surgery gathering, stooping and stomping into the room like a heron with a prolapse, muttering about how unfair her life was and that she really deserved more holiday than anyone else since at her height her organs were forced to work that much harder, making her much more tired than anyone else, and so making it more difficult for her to relax adequately at the weekends.

Greg could not stand much more of their company, especially so early in the day, so he left for his room to settle to his desk and begin his surgery, hoping that the patients would prove less annoying than his partners.

He immediately noted that flaky skin man had somehow managed through his alcoholic daze to remember to keep his promise, and was here for his review. It was with no little intrigue that Greg called him through for his consultation.

"Hiya doc"

"Good morning sir. Thank you for coming back to see me again. Shall we get straight to it and have a look at how your skin is coming on?"

"Do ya really need to actually see it doc?"

"Well, yes I do really."

"Are you sure?"

"Well, yes, otherwise it's a little difficult to assess how it's progressing."

"But can you not just give me some more stuff?"

"No, I'm afraid I really do need to have a look."

"Shit."

With this he disrobed, revealing a most astonishing sight for Dr. Finn's early morning eyes.

"My own are all dirty doc, so I've had to wear my girlfriend's."

Greg was confronted by a fifty year old scouse alcoholic, whose skin was falling off all around him, with his groin dripping and oozing into a now sodden tiny black G-string, which was desperately struggling and failing to support his scrotum. It looked like a hammock after a storm, with one large hairy testicle hanging out over the side.

Greg took a few moments to compose himself, and whilst he did so numerous issues occurred to him whilst he considered how he should handle this situation. If you knew that you were going to see your doctor explicitly for the purpose of reviewing the condition of your skin, when he had thoroughly looked at your skin the last time, given you some treatment, and wanted to see how it was helping, was it not reasonable to expect that he would want to look at the actual skin again? Was this not fairly obvious? And so if this was the case, would it not have been possible at some point to have washed some of those dirtied undergarments, even without the added incentive of an impending doctor's appointment, so that you wouldn't have to borrow your girlfriend's in the first place? In fact, couldn't he have had a wash generally as well?

When Greg was discussing his day over a swift pint with his mate Rich, he couldn't help but describe to him the events concerning flaky skin man, in an anonymous manner of course. Greg was intrigued when Rich was hardly fazed at all by the G-string itself, but instead his first reaction was

"Bollocks! He's got a fucking girlfriend!"

It was true that Greg had missed this element as a major issue, and they now wondered what on earth had attracted someone into sharing a bed with this flaky weeping skinned, alcohol fuelled man, whilst an ever growing pile of soaked used underwear grew at an astonishing rate in the corner of the bedroom?

At least if he could get a girlfriend then there was hope for everyone, but then the natural thought progression was that she was imaginary. But then where had he found the G-string? They were both in strong agreement in fervently hoping that it wasn't from his mother.

What finally happened to this patient would forever remain a mystery to Greg, as he moved out of the practice area and so had to join another surgery. Greg supposed that he could have always just followed the skin trail to find out, but he found that his curiosity did not stretch quite as far as the skin trail itself.

The rest of the working week was spent looking forward to the weekend. Greg did not want to be in a position where he just got through the week, wishing it away, just to get to the weekend, to find that life was just passing by in a blur of mundanity, but this week was different.

Annoyingly there seemed to be an unreasonably large number of consultations pertaining to sexual issues. The main issue for Greg was that he never got it, though it seemed that everyone else certainly did, and were only too keen to discuss it openly. When you wanted to avoid an issue, to put it out of your mind, block it out, continue for a while in pleasant denial, it always seemed to come around and smash you in the face in one way or another.

Though his self confidence generally remained somewhere below sea level, he still felt that he was pretty much in his prime, kept himself in good physical condition, maintained his 31 inch waist (which made it virtually impossible to find trousers which fit ; grrr!) was not awful looking, and was not, in his own admittedly slightly biased view, a total twat.

He received the odd suggestive comment; no it was more than the odd one, it was actually relatively frequent that someone would compliment him in some way or other, it was just that it was never his own wife. In fact he strongly suspected that she was currently attempting to encourage her vagina to heal over. She seemed to get through all Greg's supply of steri-strips on a regular basis anyway.

He even saw a couple in their nineties, who were holding hands and openly talking about their ongoing and fantastic sex life, which would have been unbelievably inspiring if it wasn't for his own level of frustration. They just had to remember to take out the dentures first.

There were people whom you wouldn't think the opposite sex would go near with an extra long barge pole, whether due to their size, shape, unusual anatomy, smell or appearance, all of whom seemed to be rampant.

It was all too much for Greg and he found it spiralled inwards into a mass of frustration deep inside his mind, so miniscule yet of such powerful dark energy it could only be explained by anti-matter.

He did manage to secure his pass out for the night with the staff, but it had come at some considerable expense. Mrs. Finn had not been happy, and had only been persuaded by the prospect of a weekend away in a lavish health spa (her own suggestion), where she would, of course, need some company, and so would have to take a friend. It would not be fair for her friend to have to pay to keep her company, so Greg would have to foot the bill for them both. However, this was all well worth it to have the weekend to himself, with the extra luxury of being able to come back to an empty bed with the prospect of enjoying an immense, earth shatteringly explosive wank.

He was really looking forward to a night out; a night of freedom, where he might have the chance to relax and actually be himself without needing to pretend to be something else just to appease others. He was excited during the journey into town, and was in the pub early as usual, eager to be there. He met up with Dr. Superbus who had clearly made an even earlier start, and was currently half way down his third pint; just warming up. Dr. Dulcis soon joined them, also in an obvious cheery frame of mind at having a pass out for the night.

Neither Dr. Asper nor Dr. Rudis were coming out. They were very unlikely to do anything that might involve them actually having fun or enjoying themselves, and the prospect of relinquishing even a modicum of self control was beyond the scope of their comprehension. They would also certainly not consider socialising with "the slaves", the idea of which alone was quite a ridiculous prospect for both of them.

In fact, it was impertinent, even offensive, that they were even asked in the first place, to think that they might possibly want to be seen in public with any of the staff, or have to actually attempt a conversation. What presumption! It was unfortunate, since most of the staff were in possession of much greater personal qualities than either of them, but as you might expect, they simply didn't have the personal quality to recognise it.

People gradually arrived in the social safety of groups, and the bar filled with the hubbub of increasingly alcohol fuelled chatter. Dr. Dulcis was happily bank rolling the girls' drinks, whilst trying for a grope at every opportunity. Then in walked Emma. She radiated a halo of bright energy which seemed to infect everyone around her, giving the impression that she alone was in colour, and all others were in black and white. She was one of those rare people who drew others together, who everyone was glad to see, who enlivened the atmosphere, who just made you smile because they were so full of life.

She rolled her hips directly over to Greg, linked her arm through his and said

"Hiya Dr. Finn"

Greg almost shat himself. He was sure that this was clearly not the most endearing response to her simple hello, and had to fight desperately to try and control his body. What on earth was going on? She had only walked in and said hi, it was not as if she had asked him to do something unspeakably rude to her in the beer garden. He was concerned by the effect she could have on his body just by being in the near vicinity, and had never experienced such a total loss of control over his nerve fibres, senses or emotions before. He had almost lost control of his sphincters but had been able to regain it just in time to preserve his dignity.

He insisted she call him Greg again and through the magical effects of alcohol managed to calm himself to a point where he could talk in sentences again. When he spoke, she listened, which was a pleasant sensation indeed; that someone actually wants to hear what you have to say. He was not used to this. She had the most beautiful brown eyes, and she seemed to look with an intensity that went beyond his exterior, as if she could see deep within to his very thoughts. This was worrying, since his thoughts were not fit for polite company.

She was a bright, shining, smiling focus of positive energy, and she was soon up on the stage with the other girls at the first opportunity, gyrating away in the most provocative manner. He wondered if this was intended to show off her figure in its best light. He hoped it was, and if so it was most effective.

Dr. Superbus was a happy drunk, bouncing up and down, rosy cheeked, grabbing anyone who would oblige. Dr. Dulcis lavished "carry on" film style innuendos with alarming frequency at all the girls, but the moment one of them turned around and said "go on then" he ran off into the corner genuinely afraid of being set upon.

At the end of the night, Greg made sure Emma was safely ensconced into a taxi. As it drove off into the night, she turned and looked at him through the back window (I mean really looked at him, with one of those looks that could knock you to the ground at twenty paces); and then blew him a kiss.

"Oh fuck, I think I'm in love" thought Greg. Some time later when he eventually emerged from his daze he was able to finally jump into a taxi of his own and head home to the empty house.

There was some talk amongst the neighbouring homes of an earthquake in the small hours of the morning, though there was nothing on the news to support this. Greg kept quiet, but felt remarkably lighter downstairs.

Sunday was most pleasing. The luxury of a day to himself, feeling energised, happy, even high in a most simple fashion. He was free to do as he wished, and so went for a long run. He always enjoyed the freedom of running. It was a time where nobody could get to him, where he was unreachable, and he liked having the time and the peace to think things over in his mind. The effect of the exertion on his body was strangely relaxing, and once he was into a rhythm he found that his stress melted away.

An hour or so later he returned feeling so much better and just relaxed, listened to some music and read a little.

Of course, he stopped enjoying himself just in time to have dinner ready for Mrs. Finn's return.

The unusual sensation of rising on a Monday morning without the usual sluggishness was quite enlightening. He didn't even mind the traffic, nor the drizzle, and it seemed that little would alter his elevated mood, his newly found euphoria.

He breezed cheerily into the surgery, wishing everyone a good morning, but was still unprepared for the glance he received from Emma which had the effect of causing a mild attack of vertigo, which caused him to stumble into the water dispenser, which caused everyone to stare at him, which caused him to blush, which caused them to laugh at him, which caused him to exit rapidly to the privacy of his own room. Fucking cause and effect.

He sat down behind his desk in a state of overwhelming confusion. His traditional English background had strongly imbued him with that sense that once you were married then that was it, no matter what. Even if you were miserable you just put up with it and carried on, eschewing any chance for deeper happiness. But then he saw so many couples who were clearly not suited to one another, who were clearly unhappy, so what was right?

There was absolutely no sensation of warmth, affection or love in his own marriage, which just left him feeling empty, discontent; alive but not really living, existing but not flourishing. He always seemed to be searching for something; thinking, dreaming, imagining, that things would be better when this happened or that happened, when the job changed, when the holiday came around, but of course it never was. It was still the same old shit in a slightly different package. Essentially it was all within himself. A deep and desperate need to feel needed, wanted and loved. Something which no level of material possessions could replace, which the enduring absence of would continue to leave his soul bereft.

No matter how hard he tried he realised that he could make neither himself nor his wife happy—really happy as in deeply content. This realisation alone brought a great sadness which was a constant companion, sometimes pushed to one side but always present.

He could debate at length with himself, moralise, try to think rationally and intelligently about the rights and wrongs, but then from where do you start? What is right and what is wrong? Should he ignore his feelings and hold fast in a marriage which was destructive since that was what was considered to be the right thing to do, which would condemn him to a life of inner discontent? Maybe he should, many people would certainly think so. But who is it that says that is the right thing to do? These are modern morals invented by our modern society, they are not absolute, and they are not universal. Surely the right thing is to be true to yourself and to your own feelings if you can be courageous enough to see them for what they are and then accept them as your own.

He had work to do and this was not getting him anywhere. Clear your head Greg and turn your mind to the job. Concentrate on the patients. To some extent it was good to have the excuse of a surgery which demanded total attention, so he could avoid addressing further the truth of his feelings.

There was a knock on the door and in walked Emma carrying a cup of tea. She smiled at him with such genuine warmth that he just melted. Again he had a feeling that she just knew everything he was thinking. She turned and swayed her hips back out of the door, leaving her scent hanging in the air to torture him further. Then he saw that she had left a note. Her mobile number and a message "meet for coffee?"

It was fortunate that he was kept extremely busy for the rest of the morning, giving him no time at all to think about anything other than the patients and their problems. He retained an ability to switch his focus entirely to what he was doing at the time; a useful quality in a doctor, especially one in the depths of his own emotional turmoil.

He saw numerous patients complaining of stress and depression, most of whom again seemed to be in far better moods than he was, but helping people to see what would help themselves was a skill which came naturally. If only he could apply the same skills to his own life.

He had a call from reception from one of the girls on the front desk to inform him that one of his last patients was causing something of a commotion in the waiting room. He was apparently a Kurdish gentleman who was currently rolling around on the waiting room floor as if in extremis. However, the receptionist had been present to witness him stroll in quite normally, register his presence at the surgery, then sit down seemingly quite content with the world, only moments before.

Greg took a deep breath and called him through to see what would happen. The patient miraculously leapt to his feet and came straight round to the room. He sat down directly and indicated that he needed an interpreter (he simply said "interpreter", quite a tricky word, so why not learn the simple ones too?). In the time it took for Greg to pick up the telephone and dial through to the interpreter service, the patient had gotten up off the chair, lay down on the floor and was currently rolling around clutching at his abdomen in a charade of apparent agony.

"Fantastic" thought Greg. He was not prepared to put up with this kind of shit any longer, so he just shouted at the patient

"No! Stop it. Just get up off the floor and sit down!"

To Greg's mild surprise the patient actually did get up off the floor and sat down. As the interpreter came onto the line, Greg turned to explain the situation. When he turned back to offer the phone to the patient, he was not there, but instead was back on the floor rolling around again.

According to the medical notes this was a recurrent theme. The patient had seen all the doctors in the surgery, been referred for further investigation to seemingly every consultant in every speciality except one—the one he refused but seemed to need the most—psychiatry.

He had undergone every possible investigation, all of which came back as expected—entirely normal. The specialists had felt obliged to run the tests but hadn't really expected to find anything wrong, but these days with the fear of litigation added to the inability to actually converse with the patient meant he received a whole batch of expensive tests he didn't really need. Anyway they were all reassuringly normal, and so he was gratefully despatched back to general practice, a fully investigated, physically normal non-English speaking man who came to the surgery at least three times a week to roll around on the floor for a while, and then point blankly refused to see a psychiatrist. So what to do? He took up a great deal of extra time simply due to the need for an interpreter, so there were consequently less appointments available for the rest of the practice's patients, and there seemed to be no obvious solution whilst he persisted in refusing some mental health input.

Greg personally escorted him off the premises, and arranged for a letter to be translated into Kurdish asking him not to return for the same problem that had already been fully investigated. The next day he was back rolling around in the waiting room again.

The rest of the week went by in a blur of too many things to do and too little time to fit them all in. He didn't even have time to eat in the day and was so tired that there was some reliance on local takeaway food which always irritated Greg, making him feel like he had failed himself. Mrs. Finn wasn't much help, and was in an even fouler mood than usual. She simply did not speak to him when he came home from work, other than to say "I'm going to bed" before slamming doors melodramatically and going to sleep around nine o'clock each evening.

Greg could only surmise that she had exhausted her vocal chords over coffee with friends each day and that when this was considered it was actually quite thoughtless of him to expect any sort of conversation from her in the first place.

The actual cause of this behaviour, as Greg well knew, was the fact that he was going away for the weekend. He had always loved to escape to the mountain regions of Britain, and indeed abroad, but these excursions had become all too infrequent, the timing coinciding with around when he got married. He had managed to secure this single weekend away with some medical school mates, the first for a year, by booking it well in advance, and only after Mrs. Finn had enjoyed a bottle of fine wine before giving her consent.

She knew that she had agreed to the weekend away but she didn't like it; not one bit. Who was going to do the damn chores? She was going to have a bloody miserable weekend stuck in a house that hadn't been cleaned, vacuumed, dusted, where the washing wasn't done, the washing up left out etc, etc. She would just have to put up with it until he got back, so he ought to show her some damn sympathy and appreciate her forbearance.

Nevertheless he was going, and even the increase in the level of grief was well worth putting up with for a weekend in the mountains. If you have a goal to aim for you can get through all sorts. A small light part way through an otherwise endless tunnel.

He had arranged to leave straight from work on the Friday evening and so was pleased when he was finally able to complete his surgery and watch the last patient leave his room, allowing him to release that end of term feeling.

The last patient had been interesting. A young man who had attended the surgery concerned that he had a clitoris. He said that he knew he had one since when he rubbed himself down there he was sure he experienced a female orgasm. Greg had to explain that perhaps it wasn't actually exactly the same as a female orgasm that he was feeling, though it was undoubtedly not unpleasant, and that he absolutely, definitely, certainly did not have a clitoris. What he did have were entirely normal male genitalia. He seemed a little incredulous that what he was feeling might be something other than a female orgasm, and was a little crestfallen that he did not possess a clitoris of his own.

Greg had a feeling that he would be off home to explore and probe the area thoroughly in further search for an elusive clitoris, that he remained certain of eventually finding.

This type of consultation seemed quite normal now for Greg. He was becoming more used to the bizarre nature of his surgeries. What was a rarity now was the unusual encounter with an English speaking, literate, polite patient with an actual genuine single medical problem; one that he could actually help. Come to think of it, wasn't that why he became a doctor in the first place?

He tidied his desk and left with a spring in his step. The girls were all aware that he was off to the mountains for the weekend, since he had mentioned it once or twice, and wished him a good trip. Emma held his gaze as he left for a moment longer than was necessary, and said

"Stay safe Dr. Finn. Have a great weekend."

He left and negotiated the car park debris with a tingling sensation all through his body, and a sense of excitement, anticipation, a sense that he was really alive. He actually laughed out loud as he pulled out of the car park to head north. A couple of hours later he was driving through majestic scenery, looking forward to a beer or two and a chance to unwind.

They were all already convened in the bar of the small hotel bed and breakfast, so Greg simply dumped his bag in the room and headed straight down to join the others. They had all been through the turmoil of medical school together, and though they now worked at diverse locations around the country, they had a strong and easy bond forged through pressures of work, exams, and subsequent junior doctor hours, that meant they were immediately comfortable in each other's company.

They had needed to rely on each other with a kind of siege mentality through endless hours on call in hospital, so their easy familiarity was welcome for Greg. He sat down with a beer in hand to find Tim in full swing remembering stories from medical school and was currently relaying an episode which occurred during a gynaecology attachment.

There had been a fellow student who had been in clinic alongside the consultant, with the intention that he would be asked to go and talk to and examine some real live patients, in the hope of actually learning something. There was just such a patient waiting (patiently) in one of the clinic rooms, no doubt a little anxious, and not feeling at their most confident or robust in that kind of setting. The consultant turned to the student and asked him to go into the room, have the lady undress, put the gown on, and then he would come through shortly to join them and proceed from there. When the consultant opened the door some minutes later, he walked in to find the poor patient lying on the examination couch—naked. The student had put the gown on himself ; over the top of his shirt and tie.

"The gown is for the patient you idiot!" said the consultant. The patient was relieved to be able to cover her nakedness after some of the most awkward minutes of her life lying on a couch in front of a nervous, embarrassed and ridiculously dressed male medical student.

The student was then supervised whilst he performed a fumbled internal examination, before being released from the mutual torture to another room to await an ego crushing humiliation (in this case deserved).

The lady confided to the nurse helping her up off the examination couch, and told her

"He put his hand up me funnel and made me tuppence bleed!" This had clearly been a traumatic experience for all concerned, including her tuppence.

The very same student seemed to have a habit of getting himself into difficult situations and the telling of this episode naturally led onto another similarly amusing and also slightly disturbing tale.

He had been put down on the rota to assist the consultant in gynaecology theatres one morning, which usually just meant holding things for a while. Now you would expect most medical students to able to manage this seemingly simple task, and most indeed were. However, some dispensation ought to be considered for the manner in which many surgeons liked to instruct their assistant,

"Hold tighter. Not that tight. No tighter. No that was before, not so tight now. No, over that way. Not that way, this way," etc, etc for the duration of the procedure, which could mean several hours. Consequently it was not unusual for students to emerge from theatre with their forearms in a state of severe spasm cursing the surgeon and their own bad fortune in having been chosen to be the assistant.

In the case of our tale, the aforementioned student presented himself at the theatres a little worse for wear, having been out the night before for several beers and a ridiculously hot curry—the kind you only have due to overwhelming peer pressure and after a certain level of intoxication. The kind you don't actually taste, rather shovel down to get to the end as quickly as possible whilst tears stream down your face. It's only much later, usually the next day, when it fully dawns on you that it has all to come out of the other end, no doubt involving excruciating pain.

Anyway, he was trying to keep his head down, out of the firing line, do the job and get through the list so that he could escape for a sleep, and prepare himself for the impending toilet torture. They were starting a laparoscopic procedure, whereby the surgeon was intending to clip the Fallopian tubes of an excessively parous woman who had finally agreed to be sterilised after her twelfth child. She was in the happy situation of being in receipt of enough child benefit, and had enough troops to overthrow a regime if she so wished, and lived in a luxurious fashion with the intention of doing so until her state pension kicked in.

Her major concern had been periods. She wasn't used to them and did not wish to have to suffer them in the future. They had eventually agreed to fit a coil which ought to maintain her period free position, and so she had eventually agreed to desist from further addition to the gene pool, her previous method of period avoidance.

It was a crucial point in the procedure, when the surgeon would open up a route through the abdominal wall for the scope to subsequently follow. The major cause of surgeon stress at this point was the risk of puncturing the bowel wall by mistake, partially because this could lead to having to revert to major open surgery for the patient, but mainly due to the embarrassment of having to ask the bowel surgeons for help. Unfortunately, just as the surgeon was creating his channel through the abdominal wall, his assistant produced an expulsion which whilst silent in nature, possessed an extremely powerful stench.

"Oh shit, I've punctured the bowel!" the surgeons realisation and worst nightmare. The next few moments were a blur of intense and concerned activity. Numerous theatre staff were busily running around sorting out equipment, preparing resuscitation treatments, and generally getting ready for emergency open surgery.

The surgeon was swearing and sweating, frantically searching around the insides of the fortunately oblivious patient with his endoscope, desperately trying to locate what must be an obvious tear in the bowel wall.

It slowly began to dawn on the student that this current situation had absolutely nothing to do with the bowel of the patient, but was everything to do with his own. He was now in somewhat of a dilemma. Emergency intervention was currently on hold. The surgeon was confused. Despite having searched and searched throughout the abdominal cavity with the utmost intensity he had been unable to find even a hint of a problem. In fact, everything seemed absolutely normal, almost as if there hadn't been a perforation at all, and continued to remain so for the rest of the carefully conducted procedure. Nevertheless, staff were poised for immediate action at the first sign of concern.

Since no harm had been done, the student decided to keep quiet. He kept quiet for the entire three days that the patient was kept in hospital under close observation, having been expected to be home the following morning. The surgeon never found an explanation for that awful faecal odour just at the time he pushed through the abdominal wall, and the student thought it best not to enlighten him.

The beer was flowing in a most enjoyable fashion when Greg remembered that he had better let Mrs. Finn know he had arrived safely. He sent a text, but paused whilst considering how many "x" to put at the end. He was only letting her know he was OK, but how many would be expected? One was definitely not enough and even two seemed weak. Four seemed excessive, so he settled for three. He knew that she knew he was only doing it because it was expected. He also knew that she was aware of his knowledge of her lack of interest anyway, but he still did it. This in itself pissed her right off. But then he knew if he had not performed the ritual, she would be even more pissed off than she was already.

She replied with a simple "OK" which if correctly interpreted actually meant "you are in big trouble when you get home you bastard. How dare you go away for the weekend and have some fun. You will pay." He experienced a moment of clarity of thought, realising what it was like for those interpreters at work, where one word represents several sentences worth and vice versa. Job done, he thought, and returned to the company of his mates.

He woke up the next morning with the familiar feeling of the first morning after any sort of escape, knowing that in his heightened excitement he had overdone it slightly with regard to alcohol. He had managed a fitful night's sleep, but nevertheless was looking forward to a hearty breakfast and a day in the mountains.

Andy had organised the weekend as always, and had done so with his usual military precision without which Greg suspected none of them would ever manage to do anything. In fact he was largely responsible for making sure the whole group stayed in touch. He was made for mountaineering with thighs like tree trunks that ate up the ground leaving everyone else struggling along in a bedraggled and sweaty wake. The day's chosen route up the mountain, however, did not necessarily allow for the varying levels of fitness, experience, confidence and nervousness that existed amongst the group, but since he was already well on his way up the mountain and out of shouting distance, there was little for it other than to man up and just follow.

Greg had been up this route before and so brought up the rear to ensure all were fine, and they proceeded up a rock face which, though it was no rock climb, was nevertheless extremely exposed and required some basic climbing moves to ascend. There was some choice language from those in the group possessing the most nervous dispositions, being as they were, in the unexpected position of facing imminent death were they to slip.

"The next time Andy suggests a walk, somebody shoot him" was typical. The situation did not improve when a typically violent mountain downpour unleashed itself, rendering the rock a slippy and confidence shattering accident waiting to happen. For Greg this was fantastic. The pull of the immense void to one side, and the cold, harsh, humbling, primeval feel of the rock under his hands. This required total focus of the mind, the exclusion of worries, stresses, and the trivia of the routine of life. He felt alert, attentive, and totally alive.

When they eventually completed their route, they were drenched, tired, and ranged from feelings of exhilaration to nervous exhaustion. They were happy to get inside the slate floored bar at the bottom of the mountain, and enjoy a well earned beer. Wilko returned from the bar with a load of beer, chuckling to himself. He had lined up the eight pints on the bar, and received his change, when the barmaid asked him if he would like a tray.

"No thanks, I've got enough to carry" There was the usual tumbleweed response, aggravated by the fact that she was Polish and hadn't understood in the first place. Being the antithesis of shy and retiring, he shrugged it off and complemented her on her magnificent rack, before returning to tell the rest all about it (the rack that is), which then served as a reminder of one of his clinical exams in medical school.

He was being assessed on his ability to take an accurate history, and perform a competent examination, but unfortunately for him had been allocated an attractive young female patient. Given his red blooded male inability to ignore the external appearance of his patient, this proved to be a significant problem for him.

After bumbling through the initial exchanges, he was desperately trying to remember the order and routine for the examination itself, and block out the continual roar of his more primeval centres. This tough, northern, rugby playing, heavy drinking man's man was transformed into an embarrassed, blushing mumbling fool by the proximity of an attractive woman.

He struggled through the initial phases of looking at her hands, taking her pulse (all the more aware of his own), her blood pressure (again . . .) and then thought "oh yes, time to listen to the heart sounds". He fumbled the stethoscope onto her chest, not really listening, more going through the motions for the sake of the watching seniors, all the while trying to think what he should do next, and desperately trying not to stare at her breasts.

"Shouldn't those bits be in your ears doctor?" said the patient, noticing the stethoscope ear pieces languishing still around his neck, and nowhere near the ears they were intended for.

At the re-sit, Wilko was fortunate to have a delightful octogenarian gentleman who knew more about his own condition than most specialists, and who guided him through the exam to a bare pass.

Wilko himself had been quite infamous at medical school. He had managed to sleep with more women than seemed feasible, which was achieved via a simple but effective tactic which only really required a strong sense of optimism. In fact that was it really. His rationale was that if you asked enough girls, eventually one of them would say yes. He asked a lot of girls.

He was the only known human to have managed to hail a taxi whilst having sex. One summer afternoon, the taxi driver was cruising along, windows down, enjoying the quiet peaceful nature of the warm, lazy weather, when he heard a loud "Ehhh!" and so pulled over looking around for his fare. But this was to no avail, since the sound was one of northern climactic triumph emanating through the open window of the adjacent house.

This less than subtle hint at his underlying disinhibition was more profoundly evident at various other occasions throughout medical school. One particular example occurred during a lecture from Professor Finchley, the archetypal neurologist, with black wavy hair, heavy dark eyebrows, and looking and stalking around the lecture theatre like the child catcher from Chitty Chitty Bang Bang. He was intimidating. He spoke with a superior sneering nasal voice, and such was his presence, his aura, that when he spoke there was absolute silence in the arena. No rustling of papers, no whispered conversation about the previous night's escapades, no snide insults to the twat sat on the row in front, no coughs, sneezes, snuffles, just silence. Rapt attention.

He was delivering a lecture on fainting.

"Have any of your loved ones ever fainted?" a rhetorical question as he stalked across the front of the room back and forth, waiting to time his next statement with perfection. Well practiced. Nobody ever replied in his lectures.

"Yeah!" The unexpected response from the midst of the student mass, which could only have come from one uncontrollable mouth. Dr. Finchley froze in his stride, and slowly turned to fix a cold stare directly at Wilko. The hunter locks onto the prey.

From under his heavy brow the corner of his eye twitched.

"What did you do . . . were you scared?"

"Yeah, I didn't know whether to stop or carry on!"

Several uncomfortable moments followed, everyone looking back and forth incredulously, unable to believe he had just said that, waiting for a backlash and trying to make sure they did not become collateral damage. Dr. Finchley's face contorted, twisted, and grew into a recognisable grin

"I'm going to have to watch you Wilkinson" and he turned his back on the students to hide his amusement. The rest of the theatre was in uproar, amidst a confusion of hilarity and relief, and it was some time before either the lecturer or the lectured were ready to resume.

It seems inevitable on the occasion of good mates getting together, especially in the context of post-adventurous pursuit, that too much alcohol will be consumed. That weekend was no exception, and indeed the beers were not so much flowing, more a kind of flash flood. Late on during the evening, someone managed to retain enough lucidity to notice that Andy had been missing for some time, and had never returned from a visit to the facilities. A search party was sent out.

Strange behaviours take place amidst the gents toilets, and require the appropriate knowledge of how one should or should not react to the circumstances. There seems to be an irresistible urge which overtakes a worryingly large proportion of men whilst standing at the urinal. Spitting. There are two predominantly favoured methods, which are undoubtedly separate and distinct, but which can be utilised in a random fashion ie. If you generally favour one method, there is no rule against deviating to the other method now and again. Nobody is going to criticise, nobody will be unduly offended. Indeed it is unlikely that anyone present will be aware of your usual method to notice your deviation in the first place. So feel free to spit away via whichever method you feel closer to at the time.

The first option is the deep, guttural, choking expulsion of what needs to be a large amount of thick phlegm, which is then launched with gusto onto the upright part of the urinal. This then serves as visual entertainment for the duration of the visit as it makes its slow progress down towards the tray at the bottom, thence to be chased and harried to the plughole by the instigators own urine stream (can only truly take place in its fullest form when no other service users stand between instigator and plughole).

The second option begins with an essential forward lean, to position the head directly above the tray, allowing a gentle oozing of phlegm to simply fall from the mouth silently, to be followed ideally by a satisfying reverberating smack as it hits the tray beneath. Of course, there remains the option of then chasing the phlegm bomb down towards the plughole with the same provisos as previously mentioned.

A further behaviour which must be adhered to in public facilities concerns the direction of ones gaze. It is absolutely essential that the direction of eyesight never veers to either side, and must remain ever fixed on a point immediately in front of oneself. Any hint of the gaze flickering to either side carries with it the serious risk of misunderstanding with the associated serious consequences including physical harm, since glimpsing someone else's penis brings with it the obvious interpretation that you're a homo.

Rituals aside, Andy was finally located by the sight of his size fourteens sticking out of the side of one of the cubicles, but all was silent. An utter lack of response greeted enquiries as to his wellbeing. In a state of having even less inhibitions than usual, Wilko decided that his health was at risk, and so climbed over the cubicle wall aided by standing on the neighbouring toilet and hoisting himself over, to find Andy in a bit of a predicament. His body had evidently needed to be rid of quite a significant build up of toxins through any and indeed every orifice, leaving him in his current state of being sat on the toilet collapsed forwards with his head on the door, and vomit between his feet. He needed help. Keen to extricate his friend from this mess, Wilko flung himself over and into the cubicle, catching the strip light as he did so, sending it crashing to the floor, leaving the entire place in absolute darkness.

It would be a year or so before either were fully recovered from the ensuing moments. The wiping of arse, the cleansing of vomit, the fumbling with clothes, all taking place in the pitch black toilet, followed by stumbling out through the horrified masses and eventually into the fresh mountain air outside.

On emerging from that particular nightmare, and with Andy having the constitution of an ox and being already recovered from his little episode, they then noticed Johnny standing by the side of the exit, urinating on the pavement. At that exact moment, slowly but surely he began to fall in the manner of a felled tree, directly into the pool of his own piss. Textbook role model behaviour.

Greg wanted to savour the drive back home; those priceless final moments of peace. However, he was only too aware of the welcome he was likely to receive. His mind wandered to a certain member of staff, and as it did so his leg involuntarily tensed, pushing his speed up over the ton. He couldn't help the surprise at how excited he felt about the prospect of seeing her again and remembered that number still burning a hole in his wallet, and elsewhere.

Even amongst those who live in Arctic regions, there is no shoulder quite as cold as that which he received on his arrival home. The frosty air was accompanied by the fitting soundtrack of a few choice swear words and some hefty door slamming. Greg ironed his clothes for the coming week, had a shower, and climbed into the vast bed where Mrs. Finn was already asleep some distance away, and went to sleep dreaming of someone else.

Monday lunch time was to be spent in another meeting. The chief executive of the primary care trust was coming to grace the practice with his lordly presence for his once every several years visit to show off his latest suit and expensive car with private number plate which should have read PR1CK.

Nevertheless, Greg was intrigued to meet the chief executive. He exuded self importance and gave the impression that he was the ruler of the entire universe, but was unfortunately lacking the vocal skills that would be fitting for such a position. Ironically the only position for which his level of articulation was perfectly suited would be if he decided to join a monastery and took a lifelong vow of silence, since he found it quite a challenge to string a sentence together. At all. However, demonstrating that he had the antithesis of an ascetic lifestyle, rendering him unlikely to take up that spot in the monastery to which his vocal skills were so well suited, he rather ostentatiously consulted his Breitling before pompously declaring the meeting open.

He spoke in the manner of a politician. That is to say as if there was a little voice in his ear telling him exactly what words to use, with the intention of making damn sure he did not even entertain the idea of trying to think for himself. Government and departmental policy spewed out robotically in a mindless, monotonous, brainwashed tone. Policies created by complete and utter idiots, convinced of their own genius, who have no idea of how to deliver health care to a population. Never mind asking the professionals, the workers, the people who are actually experts in the area, no that would be altogether too sensible by far, and would more than likely defeat the object ie. the achievement of the all important headline, and subsequent personal career progression in some other field, no matter what the consequences to the public health. What should they care, they will have moved on elsewhere with their private health insurance anyway, so fuck the rest of us.

He produced a huge, massive, gargantuan false beaming rictus of a smile to express how impressed he had been with how the practice had done so well in the nationwide drive to increase cholesterol lowering statin prescribing. The fact that any half decent doctor had already been doing this for years anyway was not noticed. However, since they had recently been plagued by enough letters to account for a moderate chunk of rainforest from the trust telling them to prescribe more, they had made an effort to ensure that every person who would benefit from statins was indeed prescribed them.

This was clearly instigated by pressure from above on the trust, who then employed a lump em all in the same bucket and assume they are all shit type of policy across the board.

The chief executive was delighted by how well they had done, having virtually every patient who would benefit now taking the drug. He also explained that there had indeed been a financial incentive, and that for doing so well they were entitled to several thousand pounds to go into the practice coffers, so very well done.

He then went on to explain that unfortunately the increased statin prescribing had taken them just over their prescribing budget for the year, and that as a consequence he would have to implicate the financial penalty for this (it's out of my hands etc, etc), which ran to several thousand pounds more than their reward for doing the job in the first place. And this was how it worked.

After a brief interlude of incredulity, Greg had to gather himself to listen in to the next instalment of genius from the king of the idiots. He wanted to discuss the local 'independent treatment centre'. These had been essentially enforced again by those other idiots in the government, who had blatantly pressurised trusts into encouraging their use. These were units set up separate from existing hospitals to cream off the easier operations.

They tended to employ cheap doctors from overseas, who had frequently not even performed that particular procedure before, and could barely communicate in English. They had limited come back if anything went wrong, only took on straight forward cases, and had nothing to do with any form of teaching or training. But they were cheap (relatively), and of course it had to work because it was a government thing. What was not publicised was how it left the local hospital with all the difficult complex cases to sort out, with the risks of complications, longer stays in hospital and limited the training of future specialists, since they could not train on the most technical procedures. All this of course made the hospital look much worse when you simply plugged in the basic figures without any actual thought process. Great for headlines.

The PCT had pre-paid a multimillion pound contract with this treatment centre (which was also quite some distance away), under the misguided auspices of the governments idea of patient choice. Another great headline. However, since most GPs realised that their patients would receive far better care in their local hospital with its highly trained specialists, and located just around the corner, there really was no 'choice' at all. It was rather like offering the Queen the 'choice' of a mid terraced house in Salford instead of Buckingham Palace.

Consequently, the centre was not performing anywhere near as many procedures as their multimillion pound contract had already overpaid for, and the chief executive was most concerned that this might be construed as somewhat of a waste of money. Of course the reason for the concern was mainly to do with his own job prospects rather than the waste of public money and poor quality of care to the population he was responsible for.

In desperation, the doctors were to be offered a financial incentive again. This time it would ironically involve removing that patient choice, by paying them to refer more patients to the independent treatment centre (which was we are told only there to offer more patient choice) in order to 'get the numbers up', and not reflect quite so poorly on the PCT.

Greg wondered what the public would think of such appallingly immoral behaviour, and such despicable use of public money. It also emerged that one of the PCT board members responsible for bullying the GPs into referring their patients to the centre had found that her husband had recently become in need of knee surgery. It was interesting how all her arguments in favour of this fantastic centre magically vanished into thin air, and on no account was her husband to be referred anywhere but the local hospital. Of course it was different for her being middle class.

Greg was disgusted by the politics. He could only surmise that such behaviour must occur not only in the department of health, but in every other government department as well. It was no wonder there was such scepticism for politics throughout the country, whereby more people would vote for who they preferred as the next pop star than the next prime minister.

At least you know what you are voting for. You don't tend to find them turning round saying "ah yes, I did say I would sing that song, but when I said that I wasn't aware of the current pop song environment, and what terrible lyrics I would inherit from my predecessor, and perhaps you mistook my words since I didn't actually promise to sing that song anyway, and I was actually always committed to my principles as a mime artist, and feel I can honestly represent my music fans to the best of my ability in such a fashion." No, you know you will get a pop song or two as promised. Integrity.

Greg thought anyone who put themselves up for election ought to be immediately disqualified for wanting it in the first place. Exclude them on the basis that their ambition and greed for self importance must inevitably cloud any judgment regarding what would be in the best interests of a population.

Unfortunately, as Greg scanned around the room, such qualities were in plentiful supply.

Greg was becoming increasingly fed up with seeing patients, which was unfortunate since that was essentially his job. He had seen a particular gentleman virtually twice a week since he had started with more or less the same complaints. Of course you could argue that perhaps he wasn't doing his job very well, but there really was no helping this chap.

He was 82 years old, and was absolutely convinced that somewhere in his body hiding away was a touch of cancer. Of course there was a good chance that as time went on he may well end up being correct, at which time he will be able to fulfil an ambition held for many years of being able to say "I told you, and you never listened". If this were indeed to materialise, if indeed he were to be found to have cancer, it would probably be the happiest moment of his life, giving him the greatest personal satisfaction he had ever managed.

He was also convinced that he had multiple and numerous insects emerging from various points on his skin. There was no chance they could be from anywhere else; they absolutely had to be popping out through his very own dermis, no matter how illogical. But then logic was not his forte. To date he had brought Greg three ladybirds, two beetles and an ant, all in small plastic containers as evidence. As far as Greg could see this was only evidence that he was quite good at catching insects.

At least he wasn't hallucinating, just delusional. Unfortunately, his wife colluded with him, probably to make her life a little less testing than it otherwise would be. Greg was convinced that she didn't really believe her husband was spewing insects out of his skin, but she wasn't going to risk an argument.

When Greg found some time between surgeries to look back through his old records, he found an immense list of total body investigations that had been performed over many years, performed no doubt with honourable intentions of trying to exclude any and every disease process, and hoping to alleviate the patients anxiety with an "all clear". Of course, this had the opposite effect. The more negative investigations he received, the more anxious he became, and the more convinced was he that there absolutely must be something very seriously wrong indeed, especially since all these tests had not managed to find out what it was.

The reality was that he was more likely to develop a cancer as a result of all the radiation he had received over the years. He had been seen for consultations at the surgery over a hundred times in the last three years alone. How were you supposed to manage this? What Greg really wanted to say was something like

"I know you are 82 years old and I respect that, but for goodness sake why can't you just grow up, stop worrying about every little niggle, which everyone gets from time to time and just enjoy your life. There are so many people who never have the privilege of living for 82 years, and yes, at some point you are going to die of something, that is inevitable. Neither I, nor anyone else can stop that, so just accept it, be grateful for what you have, and live for and enjoy every moment. Now piss off!"

Of course he couldn't do this, because no doubt he would then be the recipient of a poorly worded miss spelt delusional ranting formal complaint, which would become the highlight of the day for the patient liaison worker twiddling her thumbs until at last she got a chance to haul some doctor over some "patient rights" and "political correctness" very hot coals.

What about the rights of all the other patients who could never get appointments because of people such as this? What about Greg's right to at least some level of sanity? You couldn't say the clear and honest truth anymore for fear of reprisal, so he just continued to see him far too often and made no progress.

There was a continual and seemingly endless stream of addicts, alcoholics and disordered personalities who gradually but incessantly ground him further and further down . . . no you can't have any sleeping tablets (because I know full well that you just sell them on the street and go and buy more heroin), no you can't have any codeine tablets (ditto), no you are not actually mentally ill . . . you are just a twat.

He enjoyed the challenge of seeing patients with genuine mental illness, like the man who informed him that he was recently arrived from the planet Zaffer, with its very own language "whizzer". He would come into the room and take a seat in an entirely ordinary way, seeming familiar with the set up, as though they had similar surgeries on Zaffer, and open up with something like

"Whizzer, fizzer, mizzer, tizzer, pizzer . . . ?"

Usually, this meant "can I have a repeat prescription please" at least that was how Greg interpreted it. He could of course have been saying "I'm fucking mental, please help me" but Greg preferred to believe it was the former. His psychiatrist seemed to have things under no sense of control, but at least managed to have no control on a fairly regular basis, so that was OK.

There was another gentleman who lived in a care home, who came in to see Greg at the surgery to ask if it was OK to have his shower at 10:15am rather than his usual 10am. Greg assured him that it would be absolutely fine, before reflecting on his medical genius. It took quite some training to answer such questions, and they required appropriate seriousness of mind when answering.

This happened several times but all with minor variations on the timing, each time producing the same advice. Then there was a change

"Would it be alright for me to masturbate doctor?"

"Yes, that would be fine"

"Are you sure doctor?"

"Yes, I'm sure"

He thanked the doctor, then as he was leaving Greg was seized by a premonition, adding

"As long as you do it in private"

An image of a septuagenarian going back to the care home, sitting down in the living room surrounded by the other residents, getting out his cock and cracking one off saying "Dr. Finn said it was OK" had leapt into his head just in time (if such an image can ever be described as being just in time).

A nice lady had been struggling for many years to cope with bipolar disorder and its many ups and downs. Despite every effort from the psychiatrist it seemed impossible to find the right balance of medication which would help but not cause awful side effects.

The psychiatrist was hopeful that a new drug available for such situations might help, and in agreement with Greg and the patient decided to give it a try. The patient later explained to Greg that her mother had died unexpectedly at the young age of 52 years. On her death certificate it said "sudden unexplained death".

As she opened the information leaflet accompanying her new medication, she noted the long list of side effects and thought it prudent to be aware of these before starting this new treatment of which so much was hoped. The list of side effects read as follows

"nausea, rashes, sudden unexplained death, headache, diarrhoea" etc, etc.

Nestling happily between rashes and headache, that equally common and unconcerning symptom of sudden unexplained death. There could be no greater example on the planet of a drug company covering its own arse. Needless to say the patient was unable to have complete confidence in the drug once she had read this, and so struggled on without.

The week ended with a final consultation at around 6:30 Friday evening, which happened to be a joint appointment with one of the practice nurses. Greg was not over enamoured with the reason. He was going to have to perform a vaginal examination on a 30 year old lady recently arrived in the country from Pakistan. Not as part of the immigration process; she had had some irregular bleeding which he needed to investigate. This was not really the end to the week he was hoping for, and he struggled to motivate himself to gain the correct mind set for such an intimate examination.

The nurse already had the patient prepared and ready. He put his gloves on, looked down, but was unable to see any actual anatomy, due to the vast amount of thick black hair obscuring the area. It looked like an animal had nestled down for a sleep. What an end to a crap week he thought, before saying to the patient

"Excuse me madam, can you fart and give me a clue?"

Driving home, Greg experienced a strange mixture of elation and dread which was becoming increasingly familiar, especially on a Friday. Elation at the prospect of two days away from the insanity of his work, and dread at the prospect of two days of insanity from his wife.

What he needed was some kind of release from it all, some kind of escape. Perhaps alcohol was the answer. An evening spent quietly drinking a decent bottle of wine he had resting in the garage for just such a moment. With luck Mrs. Finn would be in her usual uncommunicative introspective mood, and would retire to bed around eight, leaving him a few blissful hours without anyone trying to get something from him. He might even get to watch some sport . . . no, don't speak it, don't even think it; not yet, not until it actually happens, so precious is the idea.

He opened the front door to be greeted by an onslaught. Loud music (by someone he didn't even like very much) and raucousness, suggesting that perhaps Mrs. Finn was not entirely alone. This was confirmed by the sound of laughter. Multiple feminine voices. Shit.

He gingerly moved through the kitchen discovering as he went along the remnants of various extra large packets of crisps with ridiculous flavours like 'caviar with Sicilian lemon' and others flavoured simply with the salt from the thighs of Philippino virgins, now lying discarded and empty amidst a range of dips and sauces spread over the kitchen table.

Also present were a number of bottles of wine. All empty. They used to represent his collection of nice wine being saved for special occasions, and included the very one he had intended to consume himself that evening. Now gone.

Mrs. Finn was outside with a group of people Greg half knew doing something very odd indeed. She appeared to be enjoying herself.

"It's about time. We've been waiting for you to cook us some dinner"

Greg felt like he might actually explode. He set his mind to the task of resisting spontaneous combustion, not wanting to give them the satisfaction, or the prospect of a nice fire to sit around. He took the brave option of feigning illness, and took himself off to bed where he could seethe in private without disturbing anyone, as well as listen in to their conversation through the window.

"He's bloody useless. He doesn't do anything."

"He could at least have made us dinner"

"Is that all the wine he has in the house? How rude. We're stuck with drinking the cheap crap we brought round now"

"Order pizza. He can pay for it."

He eventually drifted off into a semblance of sleep much later, wondering how he had ended up here, where he absolutely detested his life.

The next morning he awoke, went off for a long run through the park, returned and showered in the guest bathroom, then went to the supermarket, had some lunch, and was just sitting down with a coffee reading some half wits opinion of the health service in the newspaper when Mrs. Finn emerged from her slumber. She was in a foul mood. Some people were just not capable of managing the morning after the night before, usually when they were the sort of people who were generally in a bad mood anyway.

She managed to convey to Greg somehow that her hangover was largely his fault, and as such what was he going to do to resolve matters for her? He brought her a coffee. She slowly emerged from her Neanderthal like state, and became capable of speech again. She then told him of a brace of outcomes from the immense piss up of the preceding evening that he was privileged to be made aware of.

The first outcome was that she was going to be staying at Megan's house that evening (great . . . no idea who Megan is but thank you Megan, you have made my day . . . maybe they could become lesbians, or is that too much to hope for? Can people just decide to do that? Please let it be true . . . like the patient who thought about giving it a go . . . please give it a go) along with Emily and Carly (shit . . . perhaps a gang of lesbians? Is that the correct term?).

They were going to meet to plan an impending trip which they had decided on last night . . . to New York. Girls only. For two weeks.

Several things occurred to Greg simultaneously, which he then had to process into some sort of rational order. Firstly there was the initial elation of two whole weeks of freedom . . . get in! Then there was the manner in which this spontaneous plan had been discussed ie. with complete contempt for what he might have to say about it all. There was no question of her going, she was going, and he ought to grateful that she was including him so thoughtfully in her plans.

Then there was the fact that no doubt he would be paying for the trip in its entirety. And finally, what he had been forced to go through just to have a weekend in the hills with his mates. How bad he had been made to feel, how much extra sympathy, shopping and general running around after her she had required to help assuage his guilt over having those precious two days, and she was heading off for two whole weeks without a nanosecond of thought or an ounce of concern for how he might feel about it. The fact that he was delighted was not the point.

All this happened within a few moments inside Greg's mind, and fortunately managed to stay just there rather than risking any foolhardy ideas of airing such thoughts publicly. He managed to respond in the expected positive fashion.

Greg needed an escape. Again. This seemed to be rather a theme at the moment. His recurring desire to get away from everything was the manifestation of his deeper unhappiness which he was currently failing to seriously address, and at present was barely allowing to enter his conscious thoughts. He was not sure he could face going there, but then he was not sure he could face not going there. He went out for a few beers with Rich to delay such inner investigations further, knowing that at least he would be guaranteed a damn good laugh, and that was something not to be sniffed at. Also if he got horrendously drunk there would be no comeback the next day. He could recover in his own way without further aggravation.

Staggering homewards in the early hours, Rich (who was a comedy aficionado) was telling Greg about an alleged classic Peter Sellors moment, where according to Rich he had apparently turned up at a friend's house in the middle of the night stark naked except for a hat, and when the friend eventually opened the front door blearily eyed awoken from sleep, he was asked

"Do you know a good tailor?"

Now Rich was keen to re-enact this scene for himself that very night, and was keen to have an accomplice. He had cunningly led Greg via a somewhat circuitous route which happened to pass the house of another of their friends. This friend had shot up the ranks, being rather brilliant at medicine and, well, life really, and currently lived in a rather smart four storey Victorian abode on a leafy side street. She had already reached consultant level and was undoubtedly the person everyone else aspired to be more like.

Feeling a good deal less inhibited than usual and in a suggestive frame of mind, Greg was persuaded that it would indeed be an excellent idea to re-enact this moment as a tribute to the great comic genius, and that Sally was absolutely certain to find it hilarious, particularly at 3am, the well known and universally agreed best time for comedy pranks.

They stripped off in the front garden of the beautifully maintained home on the quiet leafy side street, and bold as brass knocked loudly on the front door, and just to make sure shouted out her name very loudly several times. Nothing. They shouted and knocked again. Stirrings began inside, and a light came on upstairs. They prepared themselves for the delivery of the line which was a certainty for hilarity, and the light then came on in the hallway. Keys were being fumbled with in semi-awakened clumsiness, and then . . .

Two doors further down the road Sally opened her front door, peered down towards the two of them, and said

"What are you two idiots doing?"

They looked at each other with horror slowly dawning across their inebriated expressions

"Shit! It's the wrong house!"

They grabbed their clothes and dived over the hedge just as a disgruntled unknown home owner opened his door. They crawled down the road and into Sally's house whilst the neighbour was still trying to work out what was going on, and proceeded to explain their attempt at replicating comic genius.

It was not as well received as they had hoped, but then of course they hadn't quite nailed the . . . . timing.

Greg was able to laugh at his weekend antics on his way to work on Monday morning. He also reflected on how Mrs. Finn had transformed into a different person, so much so that he was tempted on several occasions to ask her what she had done with his wife. She was really quite sprightly and even cheerful at the prospect of her trip, the organisation of which had seemed to progress remarkably rapidly. They had booked flights for that coming Saturday, and would be busy all week with the preparations and much conferring over what to take with them, and what to do when they got there. There would no doubt be some of the more serious meetings regarding what shoes one couldn't possibly leave behind.

Greg was due some leave himself and since it was not the school holidays there was no problem with him taking some last minute time off himself. He had an aunt and uncle in Nairobi whom he had visited as a student years ago, but had never managed to return since Mrs. Finn refused to go. If they didn't speak English and have spotless facilities she was not going. Greg had been desperate to return there having fallen in love with Africa . . . the smell of the earth, the vibrancy, the feeling of being totally alive, and of course the wildlife. So if she was off to New York, sod it, he would go to Kenya.

Yet another meeting. The PCT had demanded this one at short notice, and since there was no agenda and no hints as to the reason, Greg thought they were probably genuinely coming just to let them know when the next one would be, before mopping their brows and retiring home blaming an exhausting day.

They were arriving at 2:30pm even though they were well aware that surgeries began at 3pm, and then proceeded to arrive 15 minutes late. The clinical director arrived unexpectedly, taking several attempts to reverse his Porsche into a large parking space. He was a GP from another practice who was supposed to be the medical representative on the board.

He was weasel faced, with receding hair, unfashionable spectacles, and a suit which was desperately trying to say

"I'm a very important man. No, really I am. Honest. Please believe me. I'm really very important indeed." Hence the Porsche. Not so much important man as ventriloquist dummy, having the chief executives forearm inserted firmly inside his rectum, in complete control of his mouth, thereby neatly bypassing his brain which was then itself free to wander off into its own version of behavioural therapy "I AM important . . . I AM important . . ."

They had appeared to inform the practice that according to the government, doctors were sending off too many referrals to the hospital. The reason they knew this was because the hospital charged a fee for each referral, and they needed to cut costs. The clinical director then proceeded to quote some research which he had blatantly just been fed, in an attempt to attach a hint of clinical consideration to this latest policy change.

This particular research was to the effect of if you don't operate on peoples hernias, it doesn't affect their lifespan, so don't refer people to hospital who have a hernia, as it is now known to be unnecessary.

Apart from the obvious points regarding quality of life, capacity to work, what it felt like to walk around all the time with a large scrotal swelling, and how they might like that themselves (but of course this wouldn't be relevant to them since they could give their local friendly surgeon a call, pay the fee and get the problem sorted before you could say "can't lift, doctor's orders"), there was a more salient point.

Greg pointed out that this particular research paper had actually been performed on a small South American tribal population, whose average life expectancy was 38 years. The relevance for drawing conclusions with regard to a British population, therefore, seemed to be non existent.

"We have to base our decisions on the best available evidence, and this is the best evidence we have at present" replied the clinical director.

"This isn't evidence. It's completely irrelevant."

"It's the best we have" (and we are going to damn well use it since it serves our motives very well for the time being until we get the next genius directive from the government).

This completely brainless waste of time had caused them all to have to start their surgeries late, but not to worry since they could catch up time by dispatching any hernias straight back out of the door now there was "nothing we can do".

Later, Greg was winding himself up into a gentle tirade regarding medical research.

There was so much of it. You virtually had to produce some sort of publication for the purposes of your curriculum vitae in order to progress in hospital medicine, a large proportion of which was useless, and could even be counter productive. Some people didn't care what they did as long as they got their name in print and moved on to the job they were after, and others were desperate to make the next big breakthrough.

Greg remembered his old research registrar in gastroenterology, whose name could most conveniently be easily converted to 'Dick Shite' without too many letter changes, who would breeze arrogantly onto the ward shouting for his minions,

"Boys, boys, boys! Where are my YTS boys?" Greg and his mate Kai would roll their eyes, tag along for the ward round for massive egos, and take the piss behind his back.

"What we need is a diagnosis boys, ha ha!"

"No shit, Shite"

There was a large board as you entered the ward displaying photos and names of all the staff that patients and relatives might encounter during their time on the ward. There was a picture of the irritating research registrar, explaining his current position. Greg and Kai could not refuse the opportunity to alter the entry to "researching the art of self colonoscopy".

The thing with research at the end of the day was that only a small proportion of the thousands of publications each year were of much real value. He knew this, because someone had researched it.

The week proved to be difficult again. The demand for appointments was insatiable, exacerbated by the effects of modern life, poor diets, lack of exercise, lack of sleep, stress, expectation levels, unreasonable demands, bizarre requests in the name of religious belief, language barriers, personality disorders, combined with idiotic government interference, targets, box ticking and hoop jumping. Greg was irritable and fed up. He was suffering from his own array of multiple symptoms which he so loathed when patients churned them out to him in surgery. Headaches, backache, couldn't sleep, exhaustion, painful spots all over his hairy arse from sitting at the computer for hours on end, and so on. He was losing patience with patients.

Friday afternoon a couple came into his room, sat down, and the first thing they said to him most bizarrely was "we are Christians doctor". Obviously this in itself is not necessarily a bizarre thing to say, but in the right context. As an opening gambit in a medical consultation it had him worried.

They had apparently been trying to conceive for many years but unfortunately had not been successful. Greg asked them some general questions to explore any potential reason for their difficulty, making sure there was no obvious medical cause, but there was nothing that seemed to be a particular issue from his initial questioning. He proceeded to the sometimes slightly awkward area of asking them if they had noticed any problems or difficulties with the act itself.

"Well doctor, she's never very sure if I'm actually in or not"

"Oh for fucks sake" thought Greg. Trying to keep some of the exasperation from his expression he thought about how he ought to proceed with the consultation from here. He decided to arrange some basic investigations which would need to be done anyway, and then review the pair of them when he had the results available, allowing him to arrange for them to have a longer consultation. This way he could think about how to approach the problem and be prepared to delve deeper into whether they needed to delve deeper.

As he began to explain this management plan, the woman said to him

"Be careful doctor, don't use any medical type of words or else he will faint"

"What?"

"He faints at anything medical doctor. He can't stand the sound of the words or the thought of anything like that"

"I see. Well look, we'll just start off then by doing a simple semen analysis" said

Greg, thinking this would be the most basic of tests and least likely to precipitate a problem, and reached for the appropriate form to fill in, only to be interrupted by a shout

"Doctor!" He turned to see the man slump in his chair. He had fainted. There proceeded a few uncomfortable moments for Greg, unsure whether to panic or laugh, before training took over subconsciously and he went to help the afflicted, who soon came round again and apologised saying

"I'm sorry I just went when you said those words doctor"

"Crikey!" thought Greg, "if he faints at the thought of a semen analysis it's no wonder he can't get her pregnant".

They went on their way looking horrified at the thought of him having to masturbate into a pot, and Greg wondered if they would come back at all. He also wondered whether God was trying to tell them something.

Greg was sat alone in the living room. It was Saturday afternoon, and he was enjoying the unusual calm that had settled on the house. He was relieved to have some time away from the job that he had grown exponentially to despise, and time away from his wife who was currently 30,000 feet over the Atlantic on her way to New York.

He was flying the next day. In his usual slightly obsessive compulsive way he had already packed and organised everything he needed well ahead of time and was wondering what to do with the rest of the day. It was one of those situations where there were so many things he could think of that he would love to do if he ever got some free time that he just didn't know where to start. He became mildly stressed trying to decide how best to utilise this precious time and became more so as the time drifted away and he was no longer able to do some of the things he wanted to because there was no longer enough time left. Reflecting on the ridiculous nature of getting stressed over how best to enjoy oneself for a while, he realised that this was the crux of the problem. If you never give yourself the time to do things you enjoy, life can be pretty shit.

His mind wandered in a different direction. Before he fully realised what he was doing, his thumb had danced around the buttons of his mobile phone and it was now too late. There it was as clear as day in the sent messages "would you like to meet for a drink?"

Almost immediately his phone vibrated and made him leap off the sofa. Shit the bed! He picked up the phone gingerly and read the reply, now nervous about how she would have reacted. Would she be offended, tell him to get lost and stop sexually harassing her, or worse . . . laugh. He was on edge.

"Yes, would love to. What time and where?X" He felt a rise of anxiety, fear and apprehension. How could something that was meant to be so wrong feel so right? He felt like he was hurtling through space at the speed of light with his heart racing and pounding away in his chest. He had never quite travelled at 671,000,000 miles per hour before but he imagined this was what it would feel like.

When he walked into the bar he saw her immediately. She did rather draw the attention. He scanned around nervous of seeing someone he knew before joining her, leaving her to get some drinks, then joining her again. She sensed his nerves and the reason for them, and gently took hold of his hand and looked at him calmly and deeply. He felt like she could see straight through to the very core of his being, that she could surely read his every thought. "I bloody hope not" he thought . . . she looked stunning.

It seemed to exude out of her, then filtered down her arm and into his hand, then suffused through his whole body ; an incredible sense of calm. He felt a lightening of his spirits, the lifting of a great weight, and the clearing of the storm to leave bright sunshine. He felt like his old self again, a self he had long forgotten who was now released and able to shine through. He didn't have to pretend to be anything else for the sake of someone else. He could be just plain old Greg. He felt like the ocean; deeply calm but full of life. She had achieved all of this by simply taking his hand and by the strength of her genuine open and warm gaze.

Then the words came. Like a huge flood. He hadn't realised how much he wanted to talk; to be listened to. He told her about his childhood, medical school and his marriage. How he had lost his way, barely recognised himself, how he felt like everything was just wrong. That was it, he just felt wrong.

He told her about his travels. How he had slept out on the top of a sand dune in the Sahara under that incredible, indescribably beautiful night sky. He told her about Australia, New Zealand, the Far East, North America. He had gone to Canada to spend some time studying during the elective attachment at the end of the medical school course, and had chosen there so that he could stay with some relatives who had lived in the far north in The Yukon Territory for many years. He had never met his second cousin until he emerged through arrivals at Vancouver airport and there he was clutching a photo of Greg to identify him with. They proceeded directly to a bar. Greg thought this boded well.

They sat at a table in a large bar just off the main road. It must have been around 7pm though Greg was disorientated after the extremely long flight. They had a pitcher of beer and ice hockey on the large screens around the bar, and it felt good. Then the ice hockey went off, the lights went low and onto the stage came a virtually naked woman to make the most incredible use of the pole right in front of Greg which he had barely noticed was there before. She was really rather skilled at what she was able to achieve and all of this before dinner. "Welcome to Canada" said his cousin.

He had later travelled down to America after first having to phone home to get the results of his finals. Knowing he had passed medical school, he was allowed to stay out longer until graduation a month later. He had visited San Francisco and had been on a boat doing a tour of the bay. Just as the boat passed under the Golden Gate Bridge, there was a loud thump and a splash as a body fell into the sea right beside the boat. On the lower deck, well practised deck hands took out their long handled grappling hooks and heaved the body onto the boat to take it back to the harbour. The manner in which they did so suggested that this was a common occurrence for them.

Greg had recently found out that he had passed medical school. Filled with naïve enthusiasm he went down to the lower deck to ask if he could be of help, being essentially a doctor now.

"Leave him man, he's dead"

"Well would you like me to just check?"

"Sure, if you want"

So he did. "Shit, he's got a pulse!" Then the pulse disappeared. "Double shit!" There was Greg doing CPR on the deck of the boat surrounded by sea water and diesel fumes. Japanese tourists crept down the stairs to see what was happening, and seeing the action taking place began to poke their Nikons through the rails on the stairs and started taking pictures of Greg trying to revive this bloke who had just jumped off the Golden Gate bloody bridge. He really wished he hadn't tried to be clever and just left things alone, but there was something niggling away about duties of a doctor etc etc in his mind which made him continue.

Then the lifeboat arrived. It pulled alongside and both boats were now joined and heading back to the harbour. Lifeguards then leapt across to join him with all their equipment, in a remarkably movie like scene, and they all set to work together. They shocked him. Greg could barely believe it when he saw that they actually got a pulse. They had got him back somehow. He groaned, rolled over and vomited all over Greg. The lifeguards realised they had won and started "whooping" and high fiving Greg and anyone within reach.

They raced into harbour, got the patient onto the waiting gurney and straight into the ambulance standing ready on the pier. Greg turned around to see a deck hand had fainted. He was a massive African American who looked like he could toss a buffalo for fun and was a little sheepish when he came around. He offered Greg a drink straight from a bottle of vodka, from which he took a large swig. More "whooping"; more high fives. Then that was it, everyone off the boat and on with the next tour, leaving Greg at Pier 39 surrounded by tourists, covered in sea water, diesel and vomit.

As he staggered back through the streets to the youth hostel where he was staying, he wanted to scream at everyone giving him disgusted looks "I've just saved someone's life!!" He looked very much like he was about to jump off the bridge himself.

He told her about the Grand Canyon, Las Vegas and all the travelling itself on buses and trains. He had been talking to a lady on a Greyhound bus somewhere between San Diego and Phoenix, when after around a couple of hours she decided to say to him "you've got a funny accent boy". Greg replied "I'm from England". She thought about this for a few moments trying to digest the information before replying "jeez, that's a long way to come on the bus".

He told her about Kenya; its smells, sounds, breathtaking scenery and of course the wildlife. Now he was returning it brought all the memories right back and he found he was excited to be heading back there. He loved the way Emma listened.

So many people fail to listen. He had her full attention and it made him feel more significant, more special than he could remember feeling before. They had had such different lives.

Haltingly at first, she began to tell him about her own life. She didn't feel she was worth anything, but he encouraged her, desperate to know as much as possible about her. She found this a difficult and strange concept, as people had never really bothered much about her opinion of things, but she felt she could trust him and gradually opened up despite her self-consciousness.

She had grown up locally and had fallen pregnant from her first sexual experience at 17 years old. Friends and acquaintances had found themselves in similar circumstances and gone on to have abortions but Emma was different. She knew her own mind and had the strength of character to resist pressure from others and to continue with the pregnancy. She couldn't have lived with herself otherwise.

She had to withstand a great deal of negative reactions; being judged, ostracised, the disdain, the exclusion, the barriers to future career hopes and wishes. Being gossiped about and patronised by people she didn't even know. Who the hell were they to judge what she should or shouldn't do? To her being a good mother was the most important factor. The father was never to be seen again. Her daughter Hope was now 7 years old, and Emma was entirely free of bitterness. No regrets. She had such a capacity to love, which was evident when she spoke about her daughter. Greg found he admired her immensely. Her courage, her fortitude, her inner strength and her calm acceptance were inspiring. She was a ray of sunshine.

They continued to talk, to hold hands, to look at each other as if amazed by what they saw each moment. It felt right. He knew it did because it never had before.

They kissed. A thousand tiny explosions erupted within his head and his body and he looked at her as if he had just witnessed something impossible; a miracle. Maybe he had.

Greg proceeded through the mundanities of the airport. The check in, passport control, the scanners. He had virtually to strip and point out directly the large scar on his leg hiding the metalwork within which had flummoxed the attendant with the hand held scanner who couldn't understand why Greg's leg kept buzzing. He watched on as people had their worrying looking tubes of sun cream and toothpaste confiscated. Tweezers gone in a flash, presumably in case they decided to torture the pilot by plucking his eyebrows mid flight.

He then boarded praying he wasn't seated next to some malodorous morbidly obese pathological snorer. He was delighted to find the flight was half empty and he had a spare seat next to him which proved very useful indeed as the seats were so close together that he couldn't actually sit with his legs directly in front of him. They just wouldn't fit. He had to squeeze them in at an angle, creating a most unnatural seating position which he would ordinarily have had to maintain for the next nine hours. It wasn't like he was eight feet tall either. He cursed the profit hungry bastards trying to squeeze every last fare out of the plane, but that was modern life. Squeezing everything and everywhere for more and more and more.

He had no problem with a long flight, and was actually looking forward to it. All that time to himself, to think, to be calm, to be free from bleeps, mobile phones, and people. Some space. We all need it. As it was fairly obviously some sort of crisis point in his life his thoughts turned naturally to where he was, what he had achieved, and whether he had made the right choice in opting for general practice rather than staying in hospital medicine. He had been so desperate to get out of the hospital environment he was worried he went into the community for the wrong reasons ie. to escape rather than as a positive decision.

His recent experiences had been so very negative. He thought back to his time in hospital as a junior doctor, where he had worked for three years in a variety of areas. His first job had been spent on the same ward as his house mate Kai from medical school, where bone chillingly traumatic experiences were balanced by the ability to laugh at ridiculous situations. Without the laughter, he would not have made it through. Sometimes inappropriate, sometimes hysterical, but always therapeutic, even in the darkest, blackest moments at three in the morning with some poor bastard beyond anyone's help dying on you with you unable to do anything or even comprehend the enormity of the situation in your emotionally and physically shattered state. But that was how it was day in day out, and so the release of humour allowed survival.

They befriended the ward pharmacist and persuaded him to give them vials of potent diuretic medicine, which was then poured into the coffee of their registrar. Ironically they almost wet themselves laughing so much whilst trying to count how many times he had to sprint off to the toilet for the rest of the day. He had deserved it. He had lost any empathy long ago amidst the long hours and the many horrors.

Greg had been helping him with an admission; a woman who was shitting blood and consequently required a rectal examination. She was rather large. What was really needed was a hoist but they didn't have one. They were forced to use old fashioned manpower, with three nurses holding the right leg up whilst Greg was using all his strength to keep the right buttock raised allowing a rare glimpse of an anus that hadn't seen the light of day for many years. There was trust here. If Greg were to let go, the registrar would be buried in buttock hell. At that size hygiene was not that easy either, and the registrar was in an unenviable position, crouched and gloved ready to perform the rectal exam efficiently enough to allow him to escape to fresh air and avoid falling buttock. He was all set, but then realised

"shit, I've forgotten the KY jelly!"

With all his team in extremis, and muscles straining he might not get another chance. He made a split second decision given the drastic nature of the situation, wiped his gloved finger in the moist sweaty folds of groin skin, which provided the desired lubrication to insert the finger directly into the rectum. Greg nearly vomited.

Richard Johns

It took some time for that vision to fade from his nightmares, but nevertheless he had to get on with the job. He was again assisting the registrar who had to perform a sigmoidoscopy, this time thankfully on a patient of normal weight. He watched him look closely inside the colon of this patient, moving the instrument further inside, pumping air as he went along to open up the space ahead for a better view. What a way to earn a living. Finished, he stood upright satisfied, but unbeknownst to him he had pumped a little too much air and had been concentrating so hard that he had gotten a little too close in. Greg saw the multiple small spots of faeces dotted around his face, which did wonders to counteract the self-satisfied look of a man who has just been showing off his great skills to his junior and was now waiting for the deserved adulation. He couldn't understand the look of disgust he saw

270

instead. It didn't take Greg very long to decide that he was not going to specialise in anything to do with bowels.

This feeling was re-enforced over his time in that particular job. He had been asked to help out in theatres one morning and found himself assisting one of the anaesthetists. They were in a particular theatre where a surgeon was debriding a gangrenous foot ulcer which was particularly unpleasant. There happened to be a window through to the theatre next door so they could see clearly what was going on in there, where another surgeon was crouched down with hands inside another rectum. The scene provoked the anaesthetist to remark

"That's surgery for you . . . all dead tissue and arseholes, and that's before you get to the patients."

Greg was working on the surgical admissions one day when he had to admit as an emergency a patient whose problem was one of having a carrot stuck firmly up his rectum. The carrot, much like the patient, was not for coming out. He explained to Greg that he had fallen over whilst gardening.

"Really?" said Greg. "So you were gardening naked then?"

"Er, yeah"

"With upwards growing carrots?"

It was remarkable how many different objects were removed from a seemingly insatiable flow of rectums. One could have been forgiven for thinking that it was the norm. There were just so many people who just loved to shove stuff up their arses. It was a pity they weren't more alert to the extremely difficult to predict possibility that it might disappear inside altogether and not want to come out into the light of day again without serious persuasion or indeed serious surgery.

You had to admire the ingenuity as to what people were prepared to use to get a thrill. Lemonade bottles, vacuum cleaner attachments, ketchup, upside down tea light holders (honestly), various vegetables, vibrators of course which then got sucked all the way and required dismantling inside the colon before they could be pulled out in various pieces since they were so smooth you just couldn't get a grip on them.

Greg's personal favourite episode concerned the entry of two men into the accident and emergency department very much in the fashion of a pantomime horse, draped in a white sheet. On this occasion the object stuck in the man's rectum was the fist of the chap bringing up the rear. The head of the horse had needed to be anaesthetised as his arse had spasmed around the offending fist rendering it well and truly resistant to any attempts to remove it.

Greg wished he could have been a fly on the wall for the conversation which led to them deciding to head for the emergency department.

"It won't come out!"

"It's got to!"

"I've tried everything!"

"Oh my god!"

"We are going to have to go to the hospital"

"How the fuck are we going to get there?"

"I don't know!"

"Well I don't know either!"

"We can't call your wife can we?"

"Fuck off!"

"Neither of us can drive like this"

"We'll have to call a taxi"

"No way"

"What else can we do?"

"Get a sheet"

"Yeah, that should help".

When you are young, easily influenced, especially by alcohol, and under extreme stress you sometimes do ridiculous things. That was Greg's excuse and he was sticking to it. Like when he returned with Kai in the early hours of the morning to their hospital accommodation from the local nightclub and thought, in their great alcohol inspired wisdom that it would be a great idea to call in on the ward. The night sister was a friend who was placed in a most awkward position, forced as she was to try and restrain the pair from emptying the notes out of the supermarket trolley in which they were kept, leaving them spread over the floor whilst Greg then climbed into the trolley. Off they sped around the deserted night time corridors, oblivious at the time to the multiple security cameras around the place. The subsequent few days were spent in stealth mode sneaking on and off the wards like spies trying to avoid hospital security.

It wasn't just Greg. One of his mates was working in paediatrics on the neonatal unit at the time. All the staff were nervously awaiting the birth of an extremely premature baby whose mother was currently on the neighbouring labour ward. Ah yes, the perfect time for a prank.

He placed a fake call to the unit, then hurried off en route to the labour ward. Having collected the doll and wrapped it in some sheets from the store cupboard he returned sprinting down the corridor back to the neonatal unit shouting out to the nurses for help. Horror, panic, chaos, frenzied activity all ensued . . . and then he let himself trip and fall, throwing the bundle forwards through the air towards where the nurses were gathered. They looked terrified and dived forward to try and catch the tiny bundle before it hit the floor, undoubtedly ending any chance of life for the poor baby, couldn't quite reach and had to watch as the doll smashed into pieces on the floor. This was not as well received as he had hoped.

During Greg's own stint in paediatrics he was witness to the level of vileness existing in down town scumsville when an unfortunate teenager was hospitalised with meningitis of the most aggressive nature. It had at least been picked up in time to save his life but his limbs were at great risk, leaving him confined to a hospital bed for a long stay with his arms permanently bandaged. His family seemed to run into the millions. They were ever present in some numbers doing all they could to make the ward unhygienic, noisy, and entirely lacking the calm healing atmosphere that the nurses tried so hard to promote. He was a victim of evolution, having no choice but to inherit his parents' genes. Nobody knew where half of them had come from; least of all his mother, but the half they did know about were not the best. One day after he had perhaps been on the ward for a couple of weeks, she approached the nurses station, temporarily gave the chewing gum in her mouth a moments peace and genuinely said to the assembled nurses

"He has been ere fuckin ages now with them hands bandaged up . . . he's fourteen and he's not been able to wank for weeks. Can one of you go and sort him out?" Amazing!

Another of Greg's mates was performing a Caesarean section on the very same labour ward as where the doll throwing incident was born, this time on an actual person. It was to be the first baby of a very middle class couple who were avidly watching with great anxiety everything that was going on. The kind of anxiety brought on by the belief that their lives and that of their baby were special, so much more so than the other parents to be on the ward, and so were worth more, and therefore deserved all the attention possible from all the staff available. The world actually did revolve around them. No-one else had ever had a baby before, even their parents. There was no specific reason for the Caesarean, it was just neater, cleaner and less painful this way. She found it beneath her to push a mop around the kitchen floor, so she wasn't going to try to push a person out of her vagina. Good grief no!

The child was delivered and held up for the parents to see.

"What is it, what is it?" they both cried out anxiously.

The surgeon looked around at the other staff standing nearby in the theatre in a bemused fashion, then turned back and spoke to the parents like you might try to explain something to a child

"It's a baby!" he said.

Another uncomfortable moment occurred outside the nightclub in town at the end of another night of release. All those not on call had decided to convene for a few beers and they had all emerged at around two in the morning to find an ambulance parked outside the club. This in itself was not a particularly unusual occurrence at this place.

The paramedics had attended to their patient and were about to leave, but were getting frustrated by the revellers spilling out of the club and hanging around on the road in front of their vehicle. The driver was getting himself more and more wound up. They were at work and trying to get out of there and these drunken idiots were in the way. The nature of being drunk also meant that they were less likely to be reasonable and move out of the way when asked, especially if they could see it was winding someone up. One of these people was a junior doctor called Connor who could provoke a monk into a fist fight when sober, never mind in his current state of inebriation. He began to taunt the driver regarding his portly nature, puffing out his cheeks and waddling around the street arms out wide as if he was trying to carry sheep. This enraged the paramedic driver even further, whose attention was so distracted that he forgot the other revellers, put his foot down and accelerated away . . . and ran someone over. Fortunately, the ambulance was right on hand. Connor ran away.

When Greg finished his medical job alongside Kai, the day they were leaving the ward the nurses threw Kai into the patients bath fully clothed, wallet and bleep and all. Greg was stripped down to his boxers (which were white that day, fortuitously washed) and strapped into a wheelchair, a catheter strapped to his leg, betadine poured over him to look like he had shat himself, then wheeled into the doctors mess just before lunchtime for all to see. He couldn't escape. Oh, and they had made him drink a coffee laced with diuretic. Sweet revenge. He was in agony with a bladder the size of a house before anyone would let him free.

His next job found him languishing in the depths of gynaecology for an extremely uncomfortable and miserable six months. Vagina after vagina after vagina all day long (and all night too) which was nothing like the nirvana it might appear to some folk. In the midst of self conscious, low self esteemed uncertainty this was torture.

One day he had been doing the ward round by himself, and had needed to perform an examination on one of the ladies in the bay. First on the right, in a bay with three patients on each side. He had pulled round the curtain to exclude the other five from this most intimate of examinations, and had a nurse present as chaperone and to assist. Mid examination, the patient called out cheerily to the other patients, as if she were having her nails done,

"Ooh, 'e's got 'is 'and up me funnel!" There followed raucous laughter, then blushes, then he was running off the ward . . . "I hate gynaecology!"

He spent another six months working in psychiatry. The most challenging task each morning was trying to identify who were the patients and who were the staff. They were usually all sat together by the time he arrived at 9am in the smoking room which was a constant impenetrable fog. This made the task even harder than it already was. You certainly could not rely on listening to what they had to say, since similar levels of bullshit arrived from all angles.

The ward was locked permanently, but this did not deter patients from trying to escape. Indeed one flew straight out of the window, which was, of course, on the second floor. He didn't escape very far on those two fractured ankles. He was really mad.

One night on call for the unit, Greg was called to help track down another escapee who had been thoughtful and helpful to those trying to locate him by slashing both his forearms open with a razor before running out of the unit and across the car park towards a neighbouring field. Greg and the nurses were able to simply follow the trail of blood. Elementary. Greg caught up with the patient and rugby tackled him to the ground (his most favourite moment ever at work), and held on until the lovely but gigantic Afro-Caribbean nurse reached them and literally sat on the patient, allowing Greg to let go. She handed Greg a syringe which he duly unloaded into the patient, rendering him a semi-conscious sack of potatoes—like amorphous mass which they dragged back to the unit, where Greg then stitched up his arms and lay him in a padded locked room to sleep it all off.

He played table tennis with a lad who believed that aliens had implanted a microchip into his left testicle and gave day to day news reports to update them regarding the important events. It did nothing to detract from his table tennis skills—he was really rather good.

He went out once on a home visit with his consultant to see a man who was convinced he worked for Mossad and had been found wandering around the local woods wearing night vision goggles carrying a machete.

Greg thought the best idea was probably to take up position firmly behind the two police officers present, who seemed nervous, quite young, with too tight grips on their canisters of CS gas in their sweating shaking palms behind their backs. Apparently it does work extremely effectively, but Greg couldn't help thinking that it looked like if all hell broke loose, they were standing there absolutely ready to simply deodorise the resulting carnage. Surely some massive scary looking weapon would be more reassuring all round? Especially with that machete lying there in a most sinister fashion on the coffee table next to the TV magazine.

Many entirely unsuitable relationships were struck up on the psychiatric wards, most of which were inevitably doomed to failure. This would often be when one of the couple was released back home for a while until they inevitably became crazy enough to be re-admitted, only to find that by then their estranged other half had been deemed well enough to go home for a while until they became crazy enough again . . . and so on. Two chaotic lives rarely made for one happy relationship. But it didn't stop them trying.

Greg recalled a ward round one day (which always took place in a designated comfortably furnished room off the main corridor) where each patient was discussed in turn before being called in to see the consultant. This was a multi-disciplinary meeting including nurses, social workers, occupational therapists and Greg. The nurses had kindly let Greg in on the fact that two of the patients on the ward had been caught in a compromising position the previous night in that very room and that on no account should he sit on the middle seat on the left. This was being left especially for the consultant who never saw the remaining evidence of the night's activities and sat straight down on the skid mark.

As was previously alluded to, the staff were often not much better. Greg recalled one of the nurses delighting in telling him quite openly in front of various others how she got off on watching her (clearly mental, or at least desperate and definitely deviant) boyfriend crouch over the top of their glass topped coffee table whilst she lay underneath and watched him pinch one out. He remembered thinking that really she ought not to be let off the ward herself.

Ultimately psychiatry, though interesting and often fun was not the career for Greg. Just too much of it was dealing with alcohol and drug induced problems, or personality disorders which seemed to be rife and about which you could do nothing except spend vast amounts of time trying to placate or rationalise with people who were incapable of being placated or rationalised with.

He was no clearer in his mind after all this reminiscing. All that he had experienced could make him laugh and cry, sometimes at the same time, but he couldn't see where to go from here. The hospital jobs had been tough. Long hours, politics, very greasy poles to climb, canteen food, the pressures of the work itself and the meddling of bureaucrats thrown in for good measure, balanced against all the reasons he went into medicine in the first place. Essentially to try and do some good (how awful that sounds). However, he remained demotivated by and uncertain about general practice. He cruised on in to Nairobi.

Greg emerged through arrivals to be greeted by his auntie leaping up and flinging her arms around him. This alone made him feel better. He shook hands with his uncle and they headed off to their home in Nairobi. They were both lean and tanned and worked in a private school, he as head of science, she in the administration department. They made him feel relaxed, at home and welcome. He had asked them to book him onto a back country tour of northern Kenya which left the next morning, so they tried to catch up as best they could that evening. Once he was back they would then all head off to the Masai Mara together, which they were all looking forward to very much.

Greg watched as his rucksack was strapped onto the roof of the truck, then leapt up onto the back and found a seat. The truck itself had oversized wheels giving it a high clearance for the difficult country to the north and canvas sides which were currently rolled up allowing the air to circulate freely. They were heading up past Lake Naivasha through Samburu land and then on into the desert to end up by the shores of Lake Turkana which stretched across the border into Ethiopia, before circling back around to Nairobi.

So much of his life felt fake, but this was real. The immensity of the African sky, the simple smell of the earth which alone was so evocative of something unfathomable, something ancient and intangible. The sounds from roadside huts and street vendors. It was all of the moment. Vital. He felt alive again, invigorated, inspired and moved. Tarmac ended and became dirt, rubble and sand. This was adventure.

There were not many fellow travellers on the truck, perhaps because this was going to be very basic and visit areas not so popular with tourists as with mercenaries, which was largely why Greg chose it. There was a lone man in perhaps his late thirties who looked entirely at ease with his surroundings, a young girl in her early twenties and a middle aged German couple who looked like it was just dawning on them that they had come on the wrong trip.

After a long hot dusty day they were sat around a camp fire deep in the African bush waiting for the local guides to prepare some food. They were many miles from modern facilities. If you needed the toilet you took a shovel and dug a hole. The sounds of wildlife rang out all around them. Greg had tried some basic GCSE German which had miraculously seemed to ease the tensions a little within the group, either because they were amused at how terrible he was or perhaps just because he had made the effort.

The girl slouched back in her camp chair and fiddled with a variety of piercings. She was one of those people with the kind of skin that the sun only needs to wink at for it to rapidly caramelise into a deep dark brown. The other man intrigued Greg. His name was Dominic and he was 38 years old. He had been a graduate of LSE with such flying colours and had made such positive impressions that he had a variety of offers to choose from in the city. However, his experience of that environment had shown him all he needed to know. That was not the life he would choose. In fact he detested everything to do with it, from the pin striped suits, the salaries, the bonuses, the self importance, the arrogance, to the maniacal desperation to make more and more money to whatever end. So he left London to explore the world and didn't stop. He was married with two kids aged 9 and 7 years. They all intermittently went back to England where he worked as a waiter or labourer, or whatever was going for six months or so, until they had enough to go travelling again.

They schooled the kids themselves. Who the fuck was anyone else to tell them how they should do it? His wife and kids were currently on the coast sunning themselves by the Indian Ocean waiting for Dom to join them at the end of this trip. He was doing things his own way, without hint of regret. He felt sorry for the unfortunates who worked and worked to strive towards ever more difficult targets day after day, year after year, until before they know it they are old fat and unfulfilled, with nothing in their life to inspire, to amaze, to bring joy.